Drop Dead Bread

A Laughing Loaf Bakery Mystery

Book 1

VICTORIA KAZARIAN

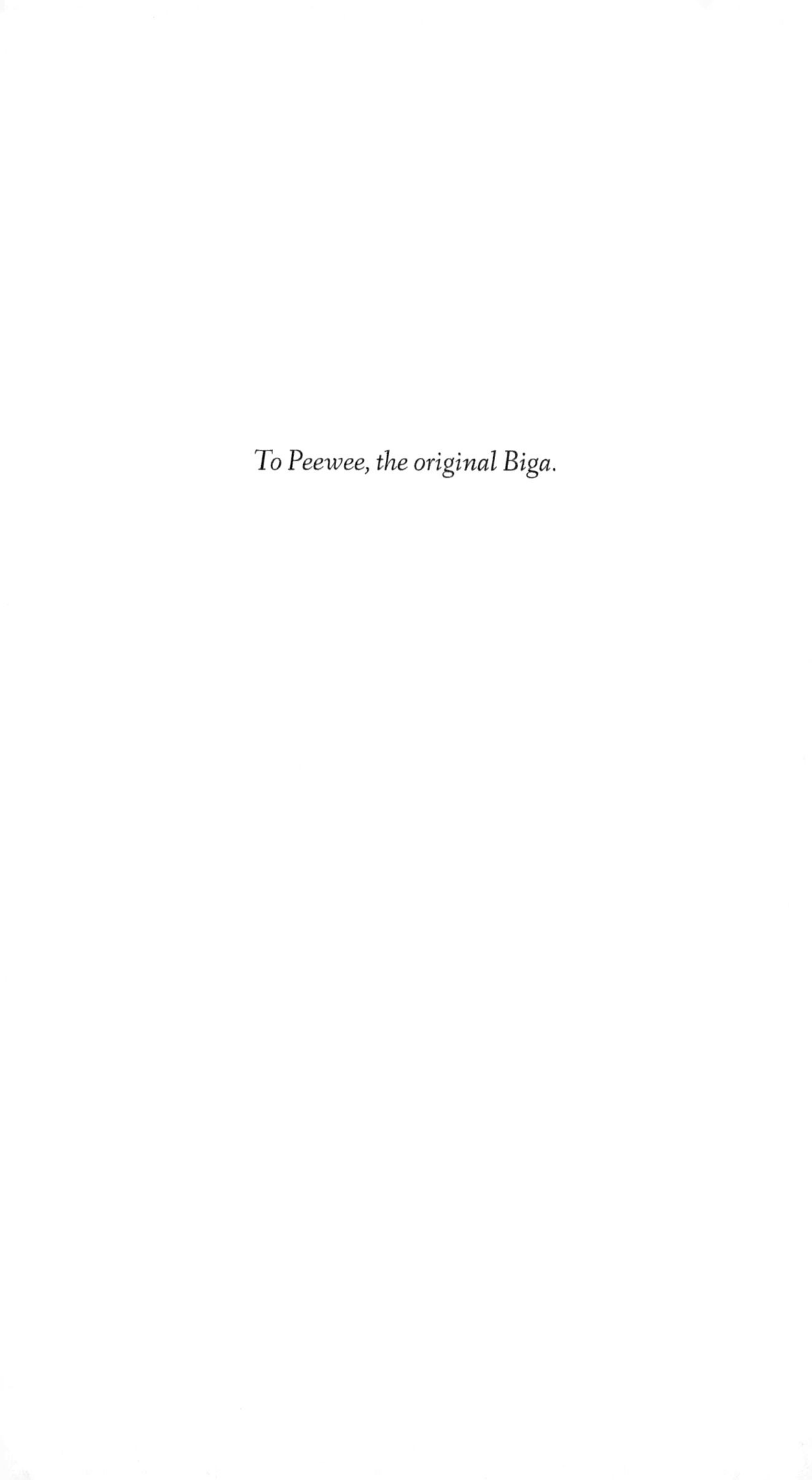

To Peewee, the original Biga.

Chapter One

The day had started out like any other day. With me, my dog, and my bakery.

At 6 a.m., I unlocked the back door of The Laughing Loaf, loaded the drip coffee machine with French roast and checked the proofer, to see all was well with my loaves of country sourdough.

I put my dog, Biga, in the gated area off the kitchen, where I could see him and he could see the customers come into the shop, without being close enough to beg them for scraps. The dog had a one-track mind when he smelled food. You'd think my little tan and brown chihuahua terrier mix was being starved to death by his cruel mistress.

As usual, I took a giant, wrapped tub of dough from the refrigerator, floured my metal baking table and began rolling the risen dough out into several rectangles to make enough cinnamon rolls to feed the morning crowd. The rich, deep smell of the yeasty dough, combined with the buttery cinnamon, caramel and brown sugar mixture heating on the stove gets me every time. I never get tired of making these rolls.

It was an overcast February day in River Grove, with

grey clouds hanging ominously over the California redwoods. Almost twelve months ago, I'd moved here from Seattle with my father, leaving a very different, much more hectic life behind.

I'd become used to River Grove mornings, with the smell of woodsmoke and fir trees and a slow, easy start to the day.

I opened The Laughing Loaf at 7:30 a.m., but most residents of River Grove didn't come in for their coffee till 8-8:30, on the way back from walking their dogs.

They lingered at the inside and outside tables, talking with each other. They discussed town business—and a good amount of gossip. The bulletin board just inside the entrance of The Laughing Loaf was papered with notices for Yoga groups, babysitters, children's clothing swaps, and benefit concerts for locals in need.

River Grove was a close-knit community. A wonderful thing. The only problem was, when I'd moved here, I'd been fleeing for my life. I hadn't planned on becoming a part of the community—or any community for that matter. All I'd wanted was a place where nobody knew me. Where I could start a life, far from the troubles I'd left behind in Seattle.

That was going to be hard in a town like River Grove, a place where everyone knew everybody.

At 7:30, the back screen door creaked open then thwacked hard against its wooden frame.

"Morning, Gracie!" Rebecca Rodriguez's lively voice rang out from the back room. "The girls produced for me yesterday. We've got eggs!"

Beck came in five days a week to help me on the morning shift. She lived a half a mile away, on a barely paved road off Highway 9, the main thoroughfare through the small towns in the Santa Cruz mountains. She'd grown up here in the mountains, and her saintly mother had home-schooled her and her four brothers from kindergarten through high school. Beck was a kind, loving, and slightly naïve twenty-two-year-old. I discovered right away—Beck would do anything to help anybody. Her husband was a cabinet installer, who left early in the morning to work on kitchen projects in Silicon Valley, twenty-five miles away.

My hands covered in flour, I turned to nod at her. "That's great, Beck. Can you preheat the oven to 350?" She set four crates of eggs on the wooden table near the fridge and headed for the oven.

I would have had no problem buying eggs for the bakery, but it made Beck so happy to contribute them. They tasted better than anything you could buy at the store, as well as being visually appealing. Any batch she brought in contained eggs in a variety of pastel hues, from light blue, to brown, to pink.

"You know you don't need to do that, Beck." I smiled at the young woman. I didn't want to take advantage of her kindness. I'd often slip "egg bonuses" into her paycheck. It was only fair to compensate her.

I rolled out my last rectangle of dough, then let it warm and rise before slathering it with a mixture of butter, brown sugar, and cinnamon.

"Want me to make you an over-medium on toast?" Beck took a couple of light blue eggs from the crate.

"Oh, God, please do." The answer flew out of my mouth, as my stomach rumbled in anticipation. The richness and creaminess of these home-grown eggs were spoiling me, and I didn't think I'd ever be able to go back to the eggs I'd bought in my local grocery store in Seattle.

I rolled up each dough rectangle, then sliced them into rounds with a sharp and very expensive knife I'd named

Andúril, after Aragorn's sword in *Lord of the Rings*. Maybe it's my background hanging out with tech people, but I'm a big nerd.

Once I slid the four pans of cinnamon rolls onto the racks of the industrial oven, I poured two mugs of French roast from the big drip coffeemaker and the two of us sat down at a table in the dining area to eat our breakfast. The egg yolk blending with the melted butter and freshly made bread was so good, I almost teared up.

What did I eat for breakfast before I came to River Grove? I can't even remember.

Beck joined me. Biga glared at us through the grill of the gate, letting us know he was mad we weren't sharing.

"We've got new neighbors on our road," Beck said excitedly, her lips curving into a smile. Life in a small town was perked up by these things, especially for Beck, an extrovert. "And it's two guys."

I was just going to ask if they were a couple, when sweet, sheltered Beck answered my question.

"They're brothers. Nate and Nico. They moved here from Los Angeles."

"That's a big change. What brings them to the mountains?" I wrapped my hands around my warm mug of coffee and watched as people passed by outside the shop window, getting their mornings started. I often got questions on why I'd moved here, when I had no previous connection to the area. It was nice to know I wasn't the only stranger in town.

"They're wildlife photographers," Beck continued. "At least Nate is. He's working on a book about birds on the coast. He and his brother are setting up an art studio behind their house, down by the creek. Nate showed Sam and I a few of the pictures he's taken already. They're beautiful."

"Maybe he'd be interested in displaying some of his

photos here." I had spent my college years in the Fremont district of Seattle studying in coffeeshops that posted the work of local artists. "He may not be ready yet, if they're still moving in, but I'd love it if he'd bring by some of their art."

Beck beamed at me. "That's a great idea. I'll ask him."

After I took the cinnamon rolls out of the oven, the caramel-cinnamon smell filled the shop. It must have extended an inviting finger out to the residents of River Grove. Residents in their flannel shirts and puffy jackets approached the shop, as if drawn by the Pied Piper of Carbs. In the cold, outside, their breath froze in clouds as they approached.

I prepared the rolls for the glass showcase, along with a tray of flaky, laminated scones, and then put out the "The Laughing Loaf Joke of the Day" on its display on the counter.

The Laughing Loaf Joke of the Day
Bacon and eggs walk into a bar and order a beer.
The bartender says, sorry, we don't serve breakfast!

After I unlocked the front door, I headed back to the kitchen to prepare the country sourdough loaves for baking. Aside from the coffee and breakfast crowd, locals would come in to buy bread and rolls throughout the day. I usually featured the country loaves along with a weekly special— olive loaf, whole wheat raisin biga, Hawaiian sweet rolls, and popular cherry chocolate sourdough, which felt more like a dessert than anything else.

The front bell on the door began jingling, a sound that I'd grown to love over the past year, in this very different new life.

The baked goods were baked, and the customers were here. The Laughing Loaf was ready for business.

Corrine Webster, town mayor, also known as Mayor C, came through the door first, her round cheeks red and blotchy from the cold outside. The yellow down jacket she wore made her look like a small fire hydrant.

"Large drip coffee and two cinnamon rolls," she said gruffly. "Make that to go, please." She had her credit card ready to insert into the pay station. "You'll do a lot of business this morning, Gracie. We've gotten a late winter chill."

Beck was already pulling out two fresh, warm rolls from the showcase with tongs and putting them in a clamshell container. I poured Corinne a large drip coffee and took the liberty of adding a dollop of oat milk, since that was the mayor's usual. I was surprised she'd forgotten to request it.

"How's your morning so far, mayor?" I asked with a smile.

"Bad." Corinne frowned. "We had a theft last night in the Speed Spot Motors yard. Catalytic converters taken from expensive cars. A Tesla was broken into. They took some paperwork. And apparently a work laptop with some classified information from a software company."

I was surprised to hear this. Speed Spot was three blocks down from The Laughing Loaf. From what I'd seen in my time here, crime in the River Grove area was usually the work of teenagers. Petty theft and vandalism.

Last spring, a group of River Grove High School students painted a less-than-flattering tribute to their vice principal on the side of the bank.

Having lived in a big city for years, I had assumed I now lived in a low-crime area. In a town where so many people knew each other, how could there be serious crime?

"The thieves came over from the valley, I'm sure."

Corinne grunted. "But it happened on our turf last night, and River Grove has to deal with it now."

The mention that tech was involved sent a shiver through me. A part of my past I thought I'd left behind when I moved here. I started to feel queasy. *Hold on, girl. Your old life is one year and nine hundred miles away. This is not your problem.*

"Any witnesses?" I asked as I pressed a plastic lid down onto the mayor's coffee.

As if to reinforce the smallness of River Grove, I heard a voice from behind Mayor Corinne—Chief of Police, Dave Westerman, also in line waiting to put in his order.

"No one heard or saw a damn thing." The white-haired man in his 60s grimaced. "The Speed Spot yard is dark at night. The only people nearby after midnight would be next door at The Riverside Bar and Grill down the alley, which doesn't close till 2 a.m. I've talked to Reggie. It was slow last night, and he and his crew heard nothing."

The mayor picked up her coffee and to-go container. "It's tough times financially for a lot of people. The platinum in those catalytic converters can bring a lot of money." She raised her eyebrows. "More reason to believe it was out-of-towners—from Santa Cruz or San Jose."

From what I'd seen in the town so far, financial struggles weren't just for out-of-towners. I'd met a few residents from River Grove, including an adjunct professor at San Jose State, who were barely making ends meet.

The mayor and police chief went out into the cold, carrying their warm goodies. Beck and I continued serving the line of customers, who were rubbing their hands together and looking at the espresso and drip machines as if they contained the elixir of life.

The next person stepped up to the counter, a tall thin

man in a tailored black jacket that looked European. A grey scarf was wrapped around his neck. He was probably a good ten years younger than me—in his early twenties. I don't use this word for any man lightly, but this guy was *gorgeous*. His light brown hair swooped down over one of his luminous blue eyes. His high cheekbones gave him a striking look. He was either an elite runway model—or a stylish Eastern European villain.

"You probably don't know how to make this up here in the mountains. I'd like a *dry* cappuccino." His slightly curled lip and bored look showed his assessment of us: we were a bunch of local yokels, unfamiliar with modern coffeemaking methods.

At the sound of his voice, Beck turned around from her spot at the espresso machine, a smile of sheer joy on her face.

"Nico Behrens! Good morning, neighbor. Yes, we serve cappuccinos. Of course, I know how to make a dry one—it means no milk poured in, just milk foam on top. I learned it watching a YouTube video."

It didn't look like Nico Behrens had been prepared for Beck's *very* upbeat voice this early in the morning. He looked at her, stunned, not quite sure how to handle this level of perkiness. His eyes darted nervously down at the floor.

The man might not have wanted to be greeted, but I shot him a friendly smile.

"Welcome to River Grove, Nico. We'll have your cappuccino at the end of the counter in just a few minutes. Thanks for coming in. It's on us."

The man slunk over to the waiting bench and took a seat. With a shake of his head, his hair resettled over his eye.

In a few minutes, the line had dwindled to two people. I

left Beck to handle the front counter and went back to start baking the country sourdough loaves. As the ovens heated, I took a bag of treats into the gated area where Biga lolled on his dog bed, distractedly drooling on a plastic squeak toy.

As soon as he saw me—or rather the treat bag in my hand—he jumped out of his dog bed, tail wagging.

"Sit, Biga." The dog walked toward me, then sat back on his haunches, a look of anticipation in his shiny black eyes. *You want me to dance? Burp the alphabet? I will do anything for that damn treat.*

I held up the dried liver treat. "Up, Biga!"

At this, Biga stood on his hind legs like a circus dog, tottering and weaving as he tried to steady himself to acquire the treat in my hand.

I let him grab it from me, and he crunched on it as he went back down on his four legs.

"That's a good boy!" Once he finished the treat, I nuzzled his face. Biga was a good companion and a constant source of entertainment. But at around twelve pounds, he wasn't going to intimidate any thieves. Unless they happened to be squirrels.

I washed my hands, then began loading the pans into the 475-degree oven. Within the hour, we'd have an assortment of fresh breads for customers coming in for loaves. I had a few round loaves of French *levain*, which I'd baked yesterday. The boules tasted better given a day or two to ripen.

My love for baking bread came from my father, who took it on as a hobby after my mother passed away when I was in high school. He took a break from his physics professorship, and we baked. He used to tell me that he was so focused on equations and theories, it was a comfort to have something earthy and tangible to sink his hands into.

Kneading dough, he said, "emptied out his brain."

Baking bread and telling really bad jokes to each other got my dad and I through three years of a really hard time. Our house smelled like a bakery most nights, and we had jars of sourdough starter all over our kitchen—our "pets." I even named them. One of them was a direct descendent of the starter used by settlers on the Oregon Trail. I called him Crusty Waggoner. It seemed to fit.

After cooling them on the racks, I brought the loaves up front on a metal cart. I loaded them into the display cabinet, on slanted, sectioned shelves, where customers could gaze on their full, browned beauty.

It never fails to amaze me: every loaf is a little miracle. You slide a wobbly slab of dough into the oven, and after the misters and heat do their work, you have a beautifully domed loaf of bread that comes out crackling softly, with a crispy, delicious crust. If I wasn't trying to stay reasonably healthy, I'd live on nothing but the stuff.

Bread, with a pat of good butter, is the ultimate comfort food. No one can tell me otherwise.

When things died down a bit, I went back to feed the sourdough starter tub. After I told Beck how I'd named our starters, she had decided this one should be called Taylor Swift. Instead of wasting the discarded starter, which is usually thrown out when the starter is replenished with more water and flour, I mixed some of it into a batch of chocolate chip cookies.

The cookies weren't traditional, but they had a creamy flavor with a tang—as if you'd mixed a dollop of sour cream into the dough. When I made these and brought them to work in Seattle, I converted the entire office to the way of sourdough starter cookies.

At 10:30 a.m., Jake Daniels from The Speed Spot came

in the door. He had the beaten-down look of someone who'd been yelled at since he'd woken up that morning. His heavy brows knitted together.

"I'll take a large Americano, Gracie. And a cinnamon roll if you've got any left."

"I heard about the thefts in the yard, Jake." Beck got the Americano going, while I pulled off two sticky spirals from the dwindling cluster of cinnamon rolls in the display. "Really sorry, Jake."

The man grimaced and shifted on his feet. He looked angry, as if he wanted to say something.

"The yard is locked, and an alarm was set." He mumbled, as I handed him his rolls in a clamshell. "Totally secure. It would be hard to get through the gates and disable the alarm. All I heard from the police chief is that the lighting we have in the yard isn't sufficient. He said it was *my* fault. Anyone who lives here knows the town shuts down at 6 p.m., except for The Riverside. There's literally no one around. What was I supposed to do?"

The Laughing Loaf had a security system, with an alarm I set whenever I left and disarmed when I came in in the morning. I'd recently installed cameras on the front and back doors. Much of my equipment—the industrial oven, refrigerator, freezer and mixer—was new or refurbished. I'd moved here from the urban center of Seattle—so I decided not to take my chances, even in a quiet community of less than 3,000 people.

But Jake, like many of River Grove's residents, had lived in the small town all his life. He was probably in his mid-fifties. He'd taken precautions, but he would have been used to a time when you didn't have to be so careful.

"I wouldn't expect to see a robbery like that in this town," I said sympathetically, as Beck set the man's Americano down at the end of the counter. "I heard a laptop was stolen with some important information on it?"

Jake wiped his face with his hand. "Oh, yeah. There's that. The car belonged to some guy who works in Santa Cruz—a Stewart Hamilton. Really dumb idea to leave it in his car. In my opinion, that's on him. But he was on a call when he dropped the car off with me to have his brakes done. I don't think he was paying much attention."

"Hope it's all recovered soon, Jake."

"Yeah, me, too." Jake flashed a grim smile, then headed down to the end of the counter to pick up his coffee. As he left the bakery, he pulled off half the roll and shoved it into his mouth. It looked like food was serving the same purpose for him today as it often did for me—comfort.

Biga looked at me wistfully as I passed by the gate. I decided to walk him home so he could spend time with my father back at the house. "Grandpa" would spoil him in the way I wouldn't be able to today. I wrapped up two cinnamon rolls for my father.

I slid Biga's harness on. He wiggled so much afterwards, full of energy and enthusiasm for getting out of his "jail," that it was hard to keep him still enough to snap on his leash.

We walked in the gravel at the side of the highway through town. Fog drifted through the tops of the redwoods on either side, giving the area a mystical feel. It wasn't raining, but the moisture in the air seeped into my jacket and made my hair feel damp. Sometimes the area reminded me of Washington state, and my senses blended nostalgia for my home with an appreciation for the unique and beautiful place I was now living in.

In half a mile, I turned onto Pilgrim Way, a short dirt road that led back to the woods. Our house was an interesting hodge-podge of architectural styles that had come about after a series of owners remodeled a vacation cabin. The front looked like a cabin, but then owners in the 1960s had added to the back to give it a living room, an expanded kitchen and two more bedrooms. They'd painted the siding on the addition a burnt sienna, as if to make it blend into the cabin front—which it did *not*. A midcentury-style carport had been attached to the side, which did not fit with the rest of the house. But, hey, on a rainy day I was happy it kept my car dry.

As I fumbled for my keys, Biga scratched at the front door. My dad opened it right away, which startled me. I don't think he'd even looked out the peephole. A wave of frustration swept through me. After all we'd been through, he should know better.

We moved into the living room, warm and toasty from the wood stove. By the way Biga ran to him, I could see I was *not* the favored human anymore. Even after throwing a treat his way today.

I looked at my dad disapprovingly as he stroked Biga's back. Of course, he didn't know what he did wrong. When he sat down in his easy chair, Biga leaped onto his lap.

"What? Why are you looking at me that way?" My dad said innocently, as he petted the dog.

"Dad, you're not supposed to open the door until you see who it is first. You wait 'till I use my key." I turned up the corner of my mouth. "We have to be careful. You need to wait until you know it's me."

"Hon, we've been here a year."

"No." I said firmly, more out of fear of what would happen to him, not me, if we slacked off on our precautions.

"But who could find us out here? The trial is over. The WITSEC coordinator told us we'd be okay."

After all we'd gone over with the federal marshals who'd prepared us for the move, he looked genuinely confused. My dad had given up his job as a popular professor at the university. He'd given up his colleagues, his quaint bungalow in West Seattle and the friends he played bridge with.

I tried to calm down as I put the cinnamon rolls on a plate for my dad, along with a strong cup of PG Tips tea. I worried about him, but I also knew he was a smart man—a man of science. He knew what he'd signed up for, but we had been here a year. Maybe he'd needed a reminder of how serious our situation was.

As I prepared to leave for the bakery, Biga jumped down off the sofa and met me at the door, his eyes baleful. He rubbed his head against my leg, as if he didn't want to leave my side. As if he didn't want me to be by myself.

"What the heck, Biga. You're a fickle dog today."

I laughed as I grabbed his leash and snapped it onto his harness.

We walked back along the San Luciano River to downtown, and soon I picked up the comforting smells of The Laughing Loaf. A reminder that I had a good life here, and anything I'd left behind–especially my lying, scumbag ex-husband–I was better off without.

At 12:30, Beck left me for the day. I could manage the register and baking setup on my own from this point. I'd shut the doors at 2, then clean up and begin prepping for tomorrow's bakes.

I was heading to the front to lock up when I heard the bell ring. Nobody who works in food service or retail is happy to see that customer who comes in right before closing time.

As I approached the door, I saw a man at the counter

wearing jeans and a rumpled sports coat. He had ginger-colored hair, and his face was red.

"I need a latte." He had a look of desperation on his face. "And anything sweet you've got. Do you have cookies?"

"I have a few sourdough chocolate chip cookies in the back." I offered. "Does that work?"

"Sure. Great." He raised his eyebrows weakly and sighed. "I've had a hell of a day."

I started up the espresso machine and headed to the back room for the cookies. I wondered if this could be the Stewart Hamilton Jake had mentioned.

"My car was broken into over at Speed Spot. Now my boss is on my case. The whole company hates me. Some pretty important stuff was stolen." His eyes were bloodshot, as if he'd been crying. "I forgot I'd left the laptop bag—I thought I could swing by to pick up my car this morning, and I'd be fine. Then I got the call from Jake. It's been hell ever since."

I shook my head sympathetically. "Hard to believe something like that could happen here."

I pulled the espresso, added the steamed milk, and passed the bag of cookies and drink to him. He handed me a ten-dollar bill and grabbed the coffee and bag with the eagerness of a man who hadn't been able to sit down and eat a decent meal all day.

"Thanks a lot. Gracie, right?" He raised the coffee cup to wave goodbye.

I was glad to finally lock the door at 2:10 and get to work on my prep for tomorrow. I wanted to finish everything before my friend Elana swung by the bakery.

Elana, the queen of good taste, was coming by with a bottle of really expensive pinot noir. It was the end of the week, and she'd just gotten a raise at her job over the hill in San Jose. We would nibble on charcuterie and drink something to celebrate. I felt honored that she'd chosen to celebrate this occasion with me. She was the closest thing I had to a best friend in town.

I'd met Elana Schiffer a few months after I arrived in River Grove. Like me, she was an outsider—someone who hadn't grown up here. She'd married Kirk Schiffer, a CFO for a tech startup down the road in Santa Cruz, and they settled in the hills above River Grove, where Kirk had lived as a child. Elana was funny, smart, and, like me, she loved to eat. I was hesitant to get to know anyone too well in town, but I enjoyed being around Elana. I had to be careful who I trusted. But as much as I tried to keep to myself, our friendship kept butting up against my new boundaries.

When Elana arrived at 4 p.m., the roll dough was doing its slow rise in the refrigerator and tomorrow's breads were rising in the warm proofer. Tables and counters had been wiped down, and I'd tallied up the day's receipts. The day was profitable; I'd sold all but two loaves.

I sliced a loaf of *levain*—French sourdough—for the board of meats and cheeses Elana was bringing to pair with the wine. I'd made some rosemary-infused butter to go with it. It smelled so good, my stomach rumbled.

I set out a pair of wine glasses. Elana and I took a table in the front dining area, along the side of the bakery, out of view of the front window. That way passersby wouldn't think we were open and try to crash our little feast.

I took the bottle from her and admired the label. "From Napa. Pretty fancy there, girl. I've heard of this winery but haven't been able to afford it."

Elana eyed the bottle like a vampire stalking its next

victim. "Me, either. But I decided it was time to celebrate. I've worked hard for this. Damn it, I deserve it."

"You do. And it's only right for me to join you." I laughed. "I couldn't make you drink it all yourself."

I uncorked the bottle and poured the pinot through an aerator, first into her glass then mine. Neither Elana nor I was willing to open this divine bottle of fermented goodness and let it sit for an hour before we drank it. An aerator would do the trick, oxidizing the wine to bring out the best of its flavors, so we could drink it right away.

"Kirk's taking me out to dinner down in Carmel on the weekend to celebrate." Elana put her nose into the glass to breathe in the bouquet, then took a sip and let the flavors circulate over her tongue. She closed her eyes. "Oh, my God. This is worth every penny."

I took a sip and sighed with pleasure. "I haven't had anything this good in years." I took a bite of one of the cheeses on the board, which paired perfectly with the lingering flavors of the wine.

"Kirk's a little distracted, unfortunately." Elana tucked into a roll of prosciutto. "One of the execs at his company had his laptop stolen last night. There was some important info on it. Potentially dangerous to the company if it got out."

I nodded and set my glass down on the table. "Stewart came by right before closing. He was pretty upset. I felt sorry for him. Apparently, he'd been grilled at work because he'd left the laptop in the car."

"Stewart was careless. He's head of engineering and he was preparing a presentation on the new product for today. He had all his data on the computer. Kirk didn't tell me the details, but there was some stuff that only management knew. Kirk said it could be devastating if it fell into the wrong hands."

A creepy wave of *déja vu* swept over me. Flashbacks to the life I left behind. I swallowed hard and Elana gave me a curious look. I quickly applied a smile to my face, the quick-save look I'd perfected over the past year.

"Elana, chances are the thief was looking for anything valuable on the lot," I said reassuringly. "They were looking for the catalytic converters and the thief happened to see a laptop and took it. Whoever has it probably has no idea what's on it."

Elana looked at me thoughtfully over her wine glass, then scooped up a blob of brie with a cracker. The dining area was getting cold, as the light of day started to fade. I pulled my sweater tighter around me.

"I hope you're right, Gracie. If the converters were taken—well, the thief was looking for things he could sell. I've been letting Kirk's worrying get to me." She brightened. "I need to be celebrating. I got top of the range on that raise. Give me some more of that wine," she ordered, tilting her glass in my direction.

I did as she told me to, then topped off my own glass. I eyed the charcuterie board. There were more meats and cheeses I wanted to try with this wine. Then I remembered Mr. Gorgeous this morning.

"On the gossipy side—Beck told me she's got new neighbors on her road." I smiled. "Two brothers. One came in for coffee this morning, not the friendliest guy. Pretty full of himself. But he looks like a male model."

"Here in River Grove?" Elana stared at me, dumbfounded. She peeled a slice of Emmenthaler off the plate with neatly manicured fingers. "You're kidding. What do these guys do for a living?"

"Beck said one of them is a wildlife photographer." I took a big sip of my full glass of wine since it seemed to be warming me up. "They moved into the house down by the river. The one that old couple sold a couple of months ago—"

"Bill and Patty Rogers." Elana sat back in her chair. "I walked through when they did an open house. It's a gorgeous place, but it's so small. And there's that strange little building down by the creek. Kind of a renovated hut—"

"They're turning that into a studio." I passed on all I'd heard from Beck.

Elana smirked. "Let's see how these city guys deal with the winter rains. Flooding along the creek. Trees falling on their driveway so they can't get out. Power outages that last three days. And, of course, *fires*. I wonder how long they'll stay." She set down her wine glass and held up her hands. "Okay, I'm being cynical. It's just that sometimes you see these people moving in who have no idea what mountain life is about. They think they've moved to this idyllic place and are getting away from it all—"

And *I* was one of those people. Though I wouldn't admit that to Elana. Life in the mountains definitely came with its challenges. I took a gulp of wine.

"I guess we'll find out, won't we?"

"At least it's some new faces in town." Elana shrugged.

I heard whimpers coming from the gated area, where Biga was taking a pre-dinner nap. He sometimes made these noises when he was dreaming.

"Let me check Biga and my loaves." I got up to make sure my puppy was doing alright. I also needed to do some slap-and-folds on my country loaves to make sure their gluten strands were stretched enough to give them a good rise in their morning bake.

First, I opened the baby-gate and went in to see that Biga had pulled his toys out and left them strewn across the linoleum floor. He lay curled up in his dog bed, burrowed under a blanket. He was still whimpering. When I came in, his eyes followed me, but he seemed afraid to move.

"Biga, sweetie." I knelt down next to him. He was shaking. I picked him up and held him close, hoping my body warmth would soothe him. The room was unusually cold, as if the heater hadn't bothered to kick in this afternoon.

I held Biga close to me and walked around the room till his shivering subsided. As I got closer to the back room, my own body started to shudder. It was freezing and felt damp.

I passed the oven, peeking in to check that the proofer was still on, and my loaves were okay. I pressed my hand against the oven door and felt the warmth.

Then I felt a flow of cold air coming at me. I looked around to see where it could be coming from. I followed the draft, and then I saw it.

The back door was partially open, and something was wedged in it. A curled, upturned hand with long fingers lay between the door and its frame. When I peered around the door and saw the rest, my stomach dropped.

There was no mistaking that face.

Lying across the back step of The Laughing Loaf was the body of Nico Behrens.

Chapter Two

Within five minutes, the police chief and his deputy arrived at the front entrance. I unlocked it, and Elana guided them through to the back.

The deputy opened the door all the way. The police chief knelt next to Nico's body.

"My guess is, he's been dead for at least an hour." Police Chief Westerman looked up, first at me, then at his deputy, Brad Castro, who nodded. "You see the color of his face?"

I did notice that Nico's skin had a slight blue tinge. But for all I knew, it could be from the cold.

"Reminds me of a poisoning case I saw up in Sac." The chief let the words hang in the air for a while.

Poison. Where? How?

Nico had gotten his coffee this morning here at a little after 8 a.m. It was almost 5 p.m. now. If he'd been poisoned by something here, it would have to be a very slow-acting poison.

"Gracie, tell me who's been in and out in the last couple

of hours." Chief Westerman stood up and started walking through the back area and alley way, looking around.

"Let's see," I said. "Beck Rodriguez, my assistant, left out the back door at 12:30." I tried to reconstruct the more mundane details of my day. "I took some trash out to the dumpster about 3 p.m. I went out to my car for some wine glasses and a tablecloth right before my friend Elana got here."

"I'm parked back there, too. I came in the back door—maybe five minutes after 4." Elana explained. "I didn't see anyone around. It was just our two cars parked back there."

Chief Westerman turned his eyes on me. He seemed to be looking right into me, searching for truth. Murder was unheard of in this small town. And now one had happened at a business owned by me, a relative newcomer. And the victim had only lived here for about a week.

"Gracie, do you know this man?"

I took another look at the high cheekbones of Nico Behrens. "I met him for the first time this morning, when he came in for coffee around 8:30. I know he and his brother had just moved in near Beck and Sam Rodriguez on Loggers Road."

The police chief nodded to his deputy. "Go talk to the brother. You know the place. The Rogers' old house."

Brad, a young man with the beginnings of a beer belly like his boss, had been born and raised in River Grove.

He nodded solemnly as he stood up. "I know it."

After he left, the ambulance and medical examiner pulled into the dirt lot behind The Laughing Loaf. The scene seemed surreal. A dead body on the back step of my bakery. A man I'd met earlier. Was it bad that I felt nothing that he was dead? He hadn't seemed like a particularly nice guy.

"Was this door locked?" The police chief looked at me. And as I thought about it, I couldn't remember. I'd taken trash out. Then brought in things from my car. Elana came in the back door at 4. I could not call to mind a mental picture of me locking that door today—which scared the heck out of me.

And here I'd just given my dad a lecture on being careful.

"I don't know if it was locked. Probably not." I didn't think Elana would have locked it when she came in. "I do have a camera on the door area, though. You'll be able to watch the video. If that helps."

The examiner spent some time with Nico's body, then waved to the EMTs. They came and loaded the body onto a stretcher, then into the back of the ambulance, which started to rumble as it prepared to leave.

I looked down at my back step, sealed off with police tape. I turned to see Elana, who'd put down her wine glass and was standing inside the entrance, her arms wrapped around herself, shivering in the cold.

"We're going to have to go over this area." The police chief said as he opened a notebook and started writing. "I'm calling in some help from the county sheriff's department. I want to go over the scene while it's fresh. If you ladies want to go inside, go ahead. But I may need to ask you some questions, Gracie. And I'll need that camera footage. We'll be here for a while."

I shot a look at Elana, who waved me back inside. Once I got to her, she hugged me.

"Okay, this sucks." She smiled ruefully. "But we've got more than half a bottle of pinot and lots of food. I say we go finish it, decompress a bit from this and carry on with our celebration."

I didn't feel great about celebrating just a hundred feet from where a man had died. Had he been trying to get inside to get away from his killer? Had he been trying to get inside to get help—from me?

The wine helped my shakiness and soothed my anxious thoughts. To distract ourselves, we talked about Elana's job, about places we'd traveled, and about our funniest childhood memories. A story she told me about accepting a dare to go into the boys' bathroom in elementary school made me laugh so hard, I thought I'd wet my pants.

It helps to laugh—something I learned as my father and I recovered from my mother's death. At the same time, thoughts buzzed through my head: Was there any connection with the thefts at Speed Spot? How did Nico end up on the back steps of my bakery? I was uneasy, still in shock, as I remembered Nico Behrens' hand reaching in through the door.

Elana called Kirk and told him she'd be home late, since she wanted to stay with me till the police chief finished and I could lock up. I decided not to call my dad. He knew I was meeting up with Elana. News of a murder at the bakery would only worry him, and I'd be home soon enough.

"This was a good idea, Elana," I admitted, as we finished off the last of the wine. "The wine and the company do help." My hunger was returning, and I grabbed a piece of salami. "It's starting to bug me now. What was this guy doing in the back alley?"

Elana was working on the last piece of manchego cheese on the board.

"That's the question," she said. "It was only our cars parked back there. You can get anywhere downtown by going down the alley—without drawing a lot of attention to yourself. We're only few blocks down the street from Speed

Spot. Do you think this was connected to the thefts last night?" Elana's eyes widened, then she sat back and laughed. "Look at us, we sound like something out of a Nancy Drew mystery."

"I always wanted Nancy's little blue convertible." I said dreamily, leaning on one arm. "I could see myself tooling around the mountains in that little coupe. In a pencil skirt and sensible low heels."

"Right? You're *so* Nancy." Elana cracked up. "I'm Bess. She always seemed to stay near the food. I believe she was referred to as *plump*."

No squeaky-clean Ned Nickerson for me, though. If my past was any indication, I was drawn to the bad boys.

"Beck will be upset when she hears about Nico's death." I changed the subject to the events of the evening. They hadn't left my mind and were hard to ignore. "The Behrens were her neighbors. And I'm sure she'll be traumatized that it happened here." I'd talk to her, though it's possible she already knew, if the deputy was at the Behrens house next door.

"I didn't see much of the guy, since I didn't look past the door." Elana spun her wine glass in her hand. "Did the police chief say something about his face being a strange color?"

"Yes, but I couldn't tell in that light." I tried to picture Nico's pale skin and high cheekbones again. "It did look a little off. Seems strange to poison him. Somebody shooting him—I could see that. Maybe he caught someone in the act of stealing a catalytic converter. Or—"

"—Maybe *Nico* was stealing them." Elana widened her eyes. I wondered if we were anywhere close with our wine-induced conversation.

"I guess it's possible," I said, not sure I wanted to

consider why this man was behind my bakery. Or the possibility that a killer was roaming the alley.

"I wonder if this will have any effect on your business." Elana's face turned serious. "Customers might stay away because they think the area is dangerous."

I frowned. I hadn't thought of that. "Oh, God. I hope not."

The Laughing Loaf had started on the track to profitability three months ago, and I didn't want anything to mess with that. I wanted to stay in River Grove—because it was a small, safe community, a good place for my dad to retire. A place for us to stay under the radar.

At 6:30, I still heard the chief and some unidentified new voices talking loudly on my back step.

Elana pushed herself back from the table. "I'm full. I'm fine to drive now. It's been a memorable evening, to say the least." She smiled as she waved from the front entrance. "I know you'll find out the scoop."

I cleaned up our table, locked the front entrance and prepared to leave for the night.

For a while, I sat in a chair in Biga's pen and held him in my lap. It was more for me than him; he just snoozed and nuzzled me. When I put him in his carrier, he didn't even fight it.

After a few minutes, I called out to the chief, who was standing in the doorway talking to a group of men in masks and gloves—probably crime scene investigators.

"Chief, call me if you have any questions. And please turn the lock when you shut the door."

The chief nodded and waved that he understood.

I walked around the building to get back to my car in the alley, weaving around the police cars and emergency vehicles.

Elana's comment about Nico's death hurting the bakery had started to bother me. Especially if I began to be associated with "suspicious outsiders" like the Behrens. I could hear Mayor C's voice: *When those out-of-towners moved here, that's when the trouble started.*

I needed answers to carry on with my life, my business.

I'd be spending some time with the chief tomorrow.

* * *

When I came in the front door of my house, Biga woke up and scratched to get out of his carrier. As soon as I opened it, he ran toward my father and leaped into his lap.

"Hey, hon—how was your time with your friend?" My father sat in his easy chair, giving Biga the attention he wanted.

I paused as I considered how to answer. How do I tell him there was a murder on the doorstep of The Laughing Loaf? If he had to ask me, that means he hadn't heard. Not telling the truth has come back to bite me several times in my life, and my life was kind of a manufactured truth as it was.

Out with it, Gracie.

"A man was found dead behind The Laughing Loaf tonight, dad."

"What?" He perked up at that. "Was it a homeless person? Someone had a heart attack?"

I flopped down on the sofa across from him and kicked off my shoes. My feet ached. I still felt a chill from standing so long at the open backdoor of the bakery, looking on and answering questions. It had been a very long day.

"They're not sure what happened to him. But he was in the bakery this morning to get coffee. Nico Behrens, who lives down by Beck and her husband. He and his brother just moved here."

"Was he old? Young?" My father wanted to know if it was someone his age, so he could calculate the probability of the same thing happening to him. He was a man of numbers.

"Young. Maybe ten years younger than me."

He frowned. "That's odd. Could it have been a drug overdose?"

For all I knew, he could be right. I knew almost nothing about the two brothers, beyond that they'd moved here a week ago from Los Angeles.

"He looked like a male model. Not that that makes him more or less likely to have had a drug overdose, I guess." Biga turned over, presenting his belly to my father to be scratched. He obliged him.

"Could it be murder?" My dad had a look of hope in his eyes. I smirked.

"Dad, are you bored here in River Grove? Is this town too quiet for you?"

He shook his head and smiled sheepishly. "River Grove is about my speed these days. It's beautiful here. The people are friendly. I do miss teaching, though."

But what if it was true? If Nico Behrens *had* been murdered? It would bring me attention I did not need. River Grove was a good choice for me because it was quiet and off the beaten path. Murder would bring the bakery to everyone's attention. It would be in the local news, if not beyond. A murder in a small town piques people's interest. After giving testimony in court back in Seattle, I didn't want to be the subject of anyone's interest.

I sat up so quickly that Biga rolled over onto his stomach

and growled. "No. It had to be drugs. Or some health condition. I'm sure it wasn't murder."

Dad smiled and took a sip of brandy, which looked very appealing to me right now. With his British accent, robe, and snifter glass, he was ready to host Masterpiece Theatre.

"I'm sure you're right, Gracie."

I went into the kitchen, took the brandy bottle out of the cupboard and poured myself less than a half an inch. I stood in the kitchen and took a few sips, feeling the liquid calm my thoughts and flow out to warm every part of my body.

I went into my study and sat down at my computer. I logged into my accounting system and went through my rundown on the bakery's expenses vs. revenue for the month so far. I'd had to call a plumber for the baking room sink, since it had backed up for the third and last time. Even with the costs for the replaced piping, my numbers still looked good.

Technology can be a force for good—keeping costs in line for the bakery business, for example—or it can be a huge distraction.

The next thing I did fell into the latter category.

I googled Nico Behrens.

Chapter Three

B y the time the sun began filtering in the windows of The Laughing Loaf, it was 6:30 a.m.

I'd woken up at 4:30. Unable to get back to sleep, I showered, dressed, and had a strong cup of coffee. I coaxed Biga into his carrier and drove in the cold pre-dawn to the bakery.

With the back entrance taped off, I took Biga in through the front. Biga wasn't pleased with this. *Silly human, this is not the way to enter the bakery.*

I set Biga up in the gated area and got a pot of coffee going. I turned on some music to keep myself moving—a playlist of 1980s Brit Pop. The first song started with a pounding bass—The Jam. "A Town Called Malice."

I was craving scones, so I made some dough, chopping ice cold butter into small cubes, then cutting them into flour with a pastry blender. After adding egg and buttermilk, I rolled out the dough with a rolling pin, folded it over and turned it 90 degrees, then rolled it out again. Once I'd done this four times, I sliced the dough down the middle, then formed it into rounds, and used a dough cutter to slice each round into triangles. I could see the layers in each scone, neat stacks of thin dough. Once baked, pockets of butter would create light, layered scones that melted in your mouth.

I was still processing the events of the night before, and the results of my Google search. Moving around, being busy, helped keep my mind focused. I baked the scones, then prepped the cinnamon rolls, letting them rise, while I got my loaves going.

In baking, timing is crucial. Slip up on your timing and you overproof your dough, ruining the crumb inside and creating stodgy, flattened loaves that people aren't going to buy. Or you bake the scones two minutes too long, spoiling their perfect, light texture.

I reflected on what I'd found out last night.

Nico Behrens was not a wildlife photographer. However, his brother Nate was. An award-winning one, who had put out a series of fancy coffee table books and even worked with British naturalist David Attenborough on a documentary.

Nico Behrens, on the other hand, had been an underwear model. And a well-paid one, too. He had appeared in numerous catalogs of high-end menswear since his debut in the business at the age of 17.

In the photos, shot in a studio with perfect lighting, Nico looked stunning. His narrow blue eyes and sculpted body were so perfect they almost looked photoshopped.

But his reality had been far from perfect.

Two years ago, he'd been accused of stealing a pair of $350,000 cufflinks at a photoshoot in Beverly Hills. The cufflinks had never been found, and Nico's story had been shaky. He'd been in the room. He'd seen the cufflinks. He'd worn them in the shoot. I saw the photo—underwear and no shirt, *only* white cuffs with the cufflinks, large, rectangular beveled diamonds in a delicate silver setting.

Only the photographer, the photographer's assistant, and Nico had been in the room during the time the cufflinks had been out—then the assistant fastened the cufflinks onto Nico on the cuffs. After the shoot, they had simply vanished.

The story had appeared in the news for months. Nico's home had been searched and his accounts examined for any unusual deposits. The photographer and his assistant had been subject to the same scrutiny. There was no sign that any of them had taken the jewels.

From the news stories, it sounded like Nico's behavior, before and after the disappearance, had cast suspicion on him. He was annoyed that the press and law enforcement kept asking him questions. His story changed—once he claimed he'd taken the cufflinks off after the shoot and placed them back in their case; another time he claimed he'd taken them off in his dressing room and told the assistant to put them away. And his partying lifestyle didn't exactly paint a picture of him as an upstanding member of the community.

Jobs became few and far between for Nico Behrens. Finally, he wasn't getting any gigs and was dropped by his agent.

As I shaped the dough for the boules, I wondered if Nate had brought his brother here to get away from the accusations. Hoping, just as I had hoped, that River Grove would be a place to start a new life.

I heard the click of the key in the front lock. Beck was here. She'd seen the police tape across the back entrance and hadn't been able to get in. I kicked myself. I should have called her last night.

I dusted my hands off and ran to meet her at the front of the shop.

As I opened the front entrance, she walked into the shop, carrying a crate of eggs, her face white.

"I saw the police tape out back. There were police cars going down our road last night. They stopped at the Behrens' place. And now this." She looked past me to the back room. "Sam was listening in on the police radios and said there was a death downtown last night. Was it one of the Behrens?"

I shot a look at the giant, antique French clock face in the dining area. 7:10 a.m. Even if we opened late, Beck needed to hear the story.

"Take a seat, Beck." I led her to a seat. "Let me get you some coffee." Though the brandy I'd downed last night was probably a better idea.

I poured her some drip coffee, with a big dash of whole milk, two teaspoons of sugar and two pumps of hazelnut syrup—coffee, Beck-style.

I carried it over to her, sat down across from her and took a deep breath.

"One of the Behrens is dead. Is that it?" She bit her lip.

I nodded. "Elana and I were sitting here. I went back to check the country loaves. It was freezing in the back room, and I saw that the back door was open. Nico Behrens was lying out on the back step, his arm in the doorway. Police Chief Westerman and Brad Castro got here quickly. They asked me and Elana questions." I shook my head. "But we hadn't heard anything while we were in here."

Beck's eyes watered up. "Do they know what killed him?"

"No. At least, last night they didn't." I gulped down the rest of my now cold coffee. "Though the police chief said

Nico's skin looked blueish and that it could be poison, but they have to run some tests."

I thought of all I'd read on the internet about Nico Behrens. Most of it was from second-rate celebrity gossip sites. It wasn't right to share what I'd read with Beck. I certainly didn't need to know it myself. But when somebody shows up dead on your back step, you get curious. Especially when they look like Nico.

I stood up. We had half an hour till customers started coming into the bakery. There was a lot to be done, and I hoped Beck would be up to it.

"Are you going to be okay?" I reached over and put my hand on her arm. Tears rolled from Beck's big, brown eyes. "I know it's a shock. He was your neighbor. If you need some time off today, you can have it. But if you're like me, work and being around people might be helpful to you today."

Beck looked down at her coffee and took a deep breath. Then she looked up at me and said firmly, "I need to be here." We both got up and went back to our jobs. I went back to the oven to put the cinnamon rolls in. Beck went to the front counter to get the coffee bar ready.

I hadn't been sure how Nico's death would affect business. But when customers began lining up outside before 8 a.m., it looked like it hadn't kept anybody away.

"Gracie, I heard about the death here last night." Susan Barnes, a woman in her sixties who ran Clip 'n Curl Salon a few doors down. "Do you think it was murder?"

Today might be full of questions I couldn't answer. "I don't know any more than you do, Susan. I'm sure the police chief will put out the news once they examine the body."

Susan sniffed. "This town used to be safe. Now with

the theft at Speed Spot, and this? Well, we're no better than San Jose."

I tried to smile sympathetically, though I thought comparing River Grove with a city of one million was a little ridiculous.

"I'm sure the police chief and his deputy will get to the bottom of things, Susan." I handed her a bag with a warm scone to go with the latte she'd ordered.

The next few customers bluntly asked who had died at the bakery and if it was murder. They wanted the salacious details. Their faces fell when I repeated that I wasn't sure—they'd have to hear more information from the police.

If anything, it looked like Nico's death on our back step was bringing *more* customers into the bakery. A horrible way to increase business, but I refused to feel guilty about it when I hadn't done anything to cause the man's death.

At 8:30, Mayor Corinne came in to order her latte. She seemed more stressed than she had been the day before.

"Give me an oat milk mocha today and an Americano, with three cinnamon rolls," Mayor C said brusquely. Beck began working on the mocha, while I pulled out the rolls and boxed them. Mayor C leaned toward me and lowered her voice. "It's going to be a hell of a day now that we've got a killer on the loose."

"I thought they didn't know for sure it was murder, Corinne." I wondered if she knew something I didn't. Judging by the look in her eyes, she thought she did. In any case, it wasn't helpful for the town's anxiety level to be told there was a killer on the loose.

She kept her voice low. "I received updates from Chief Westerman all night. Oh, it's murder all right." She cast a suspicious glance around her, then continued. "He'll make a statement after the toxicology report's in. Please keep it on the down low, Gracie."

"Of course." I handed her the box with her cinnamon rolls. She took it with her and went to wait for her drinks at the end of the counter. I saw Chief Westerman through the window, planted at an outside table, rubbing his gloved hands together in the cold, waiting for his coffee.

Of course, Beck at the espresso machine had heard the conversation. When the line had shortened a bit, she turned to me with big eyes, whispering. "So, he *was* murdered."

I shrugged. "Mayor C seems to think so. I'm interested to hear what the police chief has found out since last night." Now that I knew a little more about Nico Behrens, I wondered if the underwear model's past had caught up to him. He'd been accused of a serious felony. Maybe his death was tied to the cufflinks theft and had nothing to do with River Grove after all.

When the morning rush was over—and it *had* been a rush in River Grove terms—I poured myself another cup of drip coffee and went into the back room. I sat with Biga for a while, playing and cuddling with him. I even gave him a treat, which as usual, only made him bug me for another one.

I still felt jittery from last night. It was nice to see that the death on my doorstep hadn't kept customers away today, but there was a picture burned into my head of that hand, curled up and thrust into the back door. Like he'd been desperately reaching into the bakery trying to get my attention.

Biga caught a glimpse of the end of his own wagging tail, then growled indignantly and started chasing it. He spun around, furious at this phantom tail for taunting him.

It always cheered me up. Beck poked her head in over the gate and started giggling.

"I always thought I was a cat person, but this is so much fun to watch."

After a few minutes of entertainment, I got up, stretched, and left Biga with another treat. Then I piled a tray with the rest of the scones and brought them up front to put them in the showcase.

After I'd finished, I looked up to see a stranger at the counter. He was stocky yet tall, had a striking face and looked vaguely familiar. He was dressed like an ad for REI. Flak jacket, a thick-knit Patagonia shirt, heavy jeans, and sturdy boots that someone could hike the Himalayas in. And by the bulked-up looks of him, he'd probably done that.

"Good morning. What can I get you?" I smiled at him. He didn't smile back. Fine. Not everyone's a morning person like me.

"I'm Nate Behrens." The look on his face was more challenging than sad. "My brother died behind your bakery last night."

The light blue eyes in his tanned face pierced through me like a laser.

"I want you to tell me exactly what happened here last night. And why my brother collapsed at your back entrance, and you didn't lift a finger to help him."

Chapter Four

I stood at the counter, my hand on the espresso machine and stared. *What?*

"I didn't know he was there, Mr. Behrens." I met his stare. "I was meeting with someone in the front of the shop. I'm very sorry about your brother, but I didn't hear him."

"It happened on the premises. Right here." He set his fist down on the counter so hard it startled me. "Mr. Loudon, from the antiques store next door, told me he saw you and some woman inside, laughing when he was closing up shop. At 4:30, when my brother would have been dying, according to the police."

I bit my lower lip. This was bad optics, I had to admit.

"My friend Elana and I were drinking wine and eating an appetizer in the front dining area."

"You're telling me you didn't check the back door of your own shop at any time while you were here last night?" Nate Behrens' face was red. His eyes looked bloodshot. "He was on the back step of your bakery in the cold. Knocking on your backdoor. And you heard nothing."

"Mr. Behrens." I tried not to lash back at him. He was in pain. His brother had just died. But he'd struck a nerve. I felt a little guilty that I hadn't seen Nico till it was too late.

"Do you want to walk back with me, and I'll show you the back room? It's very hard to hear anything that goes on in there from up here. This building is old, and the walls are thick. That's why I have a camera set up on the back alley."

I looked over at Beck, who had obviously been listening to us with interest. She saw a customer come in and moved toward the espresso machine.

"Go ahead, Gracie," she said softly. "I'll take care of this."

Nate Behrens followed me as we headed to the back. Biga watched him suspiciously, letting out a deep, throaty growl as Nate passed his gated area. We passed through three doorways before reaching the back door. Nate looked around the baking and prep areas as we passed.

The back door was shut and locked, the taped-off area still visible outside the window. Nate swallowed and put his nose up to the glass. His jaw tightened.

"He was laying out on the step, and his arm was just inside the door," I said with a tremble in my voice as I remembered the sight. "I went to check my loaves in the proofer, and I felt cold air coming from somewhere, so I followed it. That's when I saw the open door."

Nate looked again out the back door window. His hands clenched into fists.

"There's no bell on your back door?" He growled contemptuously. "Or any kind of alarm?"

Yes, I had a camera, but no alarm or bell.

"So, *nobody* saw him or heard him." Nate's voice was hoarse, but still verging on angry. "Nico died and nobody heard. I still can't believe that. I can't believe he died outside your door, and you didn't hear a thing."

I knew the sound of grief well by this point in my life. I'd felt it myself when my mother had died. People who don't feel comfortable with grief often express it as anger—a fierce insistence that what happened should *not* have happened. They often look for the nearest target to pin that anger on.

"The police chief has the camera footage," I said quietly. "That may show more of what happened last night. You should talk to him."

Nate looked at me accusingly, his blue eyes focused on me in contempt. "My brother died here. He slipped and fell. You did *nothing*."

With that, he trudged back through the rooms, provoking a round of angry barking from Biga, and headed out the front door of The Laughing Loaf.

Chapter Five

"**I** want to know what you've found out."

I crossed my arms as I sat back in one of the chairs in the dining area. I'd pulled Chief Westerman over to a table after he picked up his second latte of the day.

It was 11:30 a.m. I still had to be on the lookout for customers at this point, but there wasn't likely to be many this late.

"You've given us footage from your camera. For any other information you'll have to wait for the news release like everyone else. We're waiting on the toxicology results." This seemed unfair to me since the chief had obviously passed the details on to Mayor Corinne.

"I want to know why Nico was there," I said, frustrated. "Why was he at *my* door?" Even though I knew they were unfounded, Nate Behrens' accusations had gotten to me. Guilt washed over me in periodic waves.

Maybe Nico had been calling for help. Maybe he could have been saved if I'd heard him and gotten help, instead of boozing it up and eating posh food with my friend.

"His brother told us he'd walked downtown that night." The police chief said cautiously. "He was, according to his brother—bored with small town life. He was at The Riverside midafternoon. Talked to a few people there. The bartender told us he stopped serving the guy because he was rude. We think he tried to walk home after that."

This was more than I'd expected to get from him. "Thanks for letting me know. You've told Nate this?"

"I have. He's pretty upset." Westerman grimaced.

"No kidding," I groaned. "He also wanted to see the camera footage."

The police chief and deputy looked at each other significantly. "Yeah, he asked for that," Westerman said.

Interesting. The way Westerman and Brad were trading looks, I wondered what they'd seen on the footage. I'd given Westerman the file, but I'd kept a copy on a thumb drive, just in case. If I could look at the footage, maybe I could show REI Man. I decided to think about this and revisit it tonight when my head was clearer.

At least I knew what Nico had been doing in the alley last night, and I began to feel sorry for the guy. He was just trying to get home.

Around 12:45 p.m., my monthly flour shipment showed up. Twenty-five and fifty-pound bags perched on the open back of a delivery truck. It couldn't be delivered as usual because the back entrance was still blocked off as a crime scene.

The delivery truck was double-parked in front as well, blocking the old pink Thunderbird coupe belonging to Robert Loudon, of Loudon's Antique Emporium next door.

Robert got out of his car, obviously frustrated, and slammed the door of his coupe. He threw up his hands.

"Gracie, what's going on here? I need to get my car out

immediately. I have an appointment in Santa Cruz in ten minutes."

"Let me find the driver," I looked around and found that the driver appeared to be at the counter of my bakery, talking to Beck. Judging by his smile and hand motions, he was flirting or bragging, or both.

I apologized profusely to Robert Loudon, then darted back inside and signed for the shipment, and told the delivery driver to move his truck. He could come back and set the shipment in our back room.

After 1 p.m. I was about ready to close the shop for a few minutes and walk Biga back home, since he was more of a distraction than anything else today.

My ten-pound wonder dog knew something was up, and he wanted to be part of it. He looked at everyone who came in with suspicion today. When Jake Daniels from Speed Spot came in to request a loaf, Biga growled through the gate as if he'd just remembered spotting the man on the FBI's most wanted list. I apologized to Jake, then nudged Biga away from the gate with my foot and shut the door to keep him from fixating on the man.

"Sorry about that, Jake." I brushed my hair back off my face and slipped a large boule of cherry chocolate sourdough into a Laughing Loaf bag. "Biga's a little stressed about what happened here last night. How are things going at Speed Spot? Any leads on the break-in?"

Jake let out a sigh. "No—and it seems like the police chief has found something more interesting to investigate. You ever meet that Nico guy? Really strange. Like he thought he was better than all of us." He shook his head. "Hey, I'm sorry he's dead. I know murder's a big deal and all, but I'm dealing with a serious customer trust issue. People are saying the lot isn't secure. On top of that, my son left to go back to college at the end of January. I'm short-handed right now."

Jake's face looked especially pink and mottled today and grew more so as he got agitated.

"Is there any way to put in more security measures— maybe lights on the lot? Alarms on the gates?" I asked as I handed him the bag and poured a small drip coffee for him as an extra.

Jake grabbed the coffee and loaded it up with a liberal amount of half and half from the pitcher on the counter. Then he chugged it down so fast, I wondered if he was using it to make up for lost sleep. He rubbed his eyes and set the cup down on the counter absentmindedly.

"Sure, that's what the police chief is telling me." He grunted. "But nothing like this has ever happened at Speed Spot in the thirty years I've owned it. My father started the place twenty-five years before that and passed it down to me. Of course, I'll put in some new security. I'm not stupid. But things seem to be changing in River Grove. I want to know why. I don't want to hear Westerman tell me it's my fault."

With that, Jake Daniels put his bag of sourdough under one arm and headed out the front door.

After Jake's departure, I hung a "BE BACK IN 30 MINUTES" sign with a caricature of a laughing loaf giving a thumbs up on the door.

I put on Biga's harness and leash and headed out the front, locking the door, then rattling it to make sure it was secure.

There was something about Jake Daniels' feeling mystified by his circumstances that I related to. I'd come here with the feds' assurance that this was a small town. Safe. Wholesome. Tucked away from the dangers of the outside world. I'd met good people here. And now the outside world had started to creep in, in an uncomfortable—and dangerous—way.

Biga and I made our way down the main drag, with Biga only stopping, oh, *fifteen times* to check out the local dog smells and do his business. When we got home, I unlocked the door to find my father was sitting in his chair, engrossed in a biography of inventor Nikola Tesla—next to a full cup of what I suspected was coffee he'd let sit there all morning without drinking.

I took the leash off Biga, who ran to my father's lap and nestled in. *Oh, papa, I am so glad I'm back with you. The crazy lady kept me in jail and even closed the door on me. Save me from her!*

"Any word on the murder, Gracie?" My father closed his book and took off his reading glasses. "Did the police chief have any more news this morning?"

I shook my head and plunged my hand into the bag of cashews he'd been eating and grabbed a handful. I'd missed lunch.

"The mayor hinted strongly to me that Nico Behrens had been murdered. The police chief must have told her, but he wouldn't confirm it to me." I went into the kitchen to get a bottle of sparkling water from the fridge. I returned and sat down across from him.

Biga looked at me coolly from the comfort of my father's lap. *So...you're still here. Why?*

I continued, sinking back into the couch and realizing that I couldn't relax too much here. I still had a lot to do back at the bakery.

"Nico was wandering down the alley, drunk probably. Trying to get home. His brother Nate came by today and yelled at me for not hearing Nico on the back step. He thought Nico was calling for help and that I had just ignored him. If I had heard him, I would have done something." I looked at my father with frustration.

"Of course you would, dear." My father smiled affectionately. "That's what you do." He stroked Biga. "If anything, you go out of your way to help people. And to do what's right."

Biga narrowed his eyes at me, as if he wasn't sure he agreed.

That tendency had changed my life. It had consequences, but I can't imagine having done anything differently than I did.

On my way back to the bakery, I felt unsettled. I wanted things to go back to normal. Just as Jake Daniels had said. Everything had been fine here for a year. And now all hell seemed to be breaking loose in River Grove. Maybe it was coincidence, the thefts at Speed Spot and Nico Behrens's death happening a day apart. Or maybe not.

With Biga happy and wanting to stay with my father, I walked back to the bakery after the morning fog had burned off, feeling the warmth of the sun. I took a deep breath and inhaled the musky, woody smell of the redwood trees.

That night over a year ago, Ben and I sat up in the bed, having the last conversation we'd ever have. We'd talked till 2 a.m.

I was in shock. I couldn't reconcile what I'd just found out with this man I'd known through college and married shortly afterward. A man who loved me, who cuddled on the couch with our dog. We traveled the world together, backpacking through Europe, traveling through Asia, going on safaris in Africa. He was brilliant, a whiz kid who'd excelled in school and then in the workplace. I thought the world of him.

Until the day I'd found the strange folder on his computer, labeled FANTASY FOOTBALL. With names and emails from foreign countries. And a list of amounts.

"Grace, it's not as bad as it seems. So, I have access to some information. Me and a friend from college. Technology other countries want. It's very valuable to them, in fact. Why shouldn't they have it? Technology should be shared. Look at the money as a fringe benefit to my work. It's not hurting anybody to pass it on for a price. It's not like I'm giving them information on how to build an atomic bomb."

The carelessness of his response and his admission of greed shook me.

"If you think everyone should have it, why don't you give it to them for free then?" I asked.

"Point taken," Ben said, laughing as if I were a child making a hilariously naïve comment. "You really are an innocent, aren't you?" He acted as if I were an uptight goody-goody for bringing up such a trivial matter with him. I looked at his calm, cool demeanor. He must really believe this.

He'd kept the money in a separate account, so I hadn't known. And then I'd seen the secret account information and lists of transactions – money transfers from Moscow, Shanghai and North Korea, in the folder.

"Everything we've done—the trips we've taken." His voice turned serious, with an unfamiliar sharp edge to it. "The house we've been considering on Mercer Island, with that incredible view of the lake. Do you honestly think we could afford all of this on our salaries? Are you that much of a child?"

"You can't do this, Ben. It's *wrong*." I had visions of us being arrested. Serving time in prison. My father losing his position and reputation by association with Ben and his scheme. "You were given clearances and you took advantage of them. Your employer trusted you. You need to end this now, Ben. You're putting me and my father in danger."

"Grace." He gripped my wrist so hard it hurt. "You are in this now. You have no idea how deep. You're my wife. If I go down, you're going down with me."

Suddenly the man next to me, the man I'd married was a complete stranger to me. The threatening look in his eyes was unfamiliar, and it scared me.

I'd have to play along for now. I'd tell him I'd think about what he'd told me. It made me sick to my stomach, but I told him that night, lying through my teeth, that I appreciated that he'd been thinking about our financial future and that maybe he'd had a point about technology being something that should be shared.

The next day, I cheerfully kissed Ben goodbye, shoved some clothes and my laptop with the files I'd copied in my workout bag and put my dog in his carrier. I drove a few streets away and parked. I called the FBI office and told them I needed to talk to them urgently. I called a friend of mine in Bellevue and asked if my dog and I could stay with her for a day or two.

That night Ben and his co-worker Kyle Burnett were arrested. And the next few months were a nightmare of interviews, testimonies and meetings with federal agents.

That first day in River Grove, walking with Biga among the cool, sheltering redwoods, I felt I'd just woken up from a nightmare.

The giant redwoods loomed over me.

They would be my protectors.

I would be safe here.

* * *

I walked along the road back into downtown, mentally listing what I needed to set up once I got into the bakery. I'd found blueberries on sale at a local grocery store, so blueberry scones were on the menu for tomorrow's breakfast. Then I'd mix brioche dough with the eggs Beck had brought in.

Events of the night before continued to distract me. I wanted to follow the path Nico Behrens walked that night. So instead of going to the front of The Laughing Loaf, I cut across to the alley, four blocks down the road from the bakery.

In the sunlight, I saw the backs of the shops and business on this side of downtown. There was the back deck of The Riverside, where the bartender had kicked Nico out that night. Then came Speed Spot Motor Works' back lot, where a security system company van was parked. Then the small concrete block building that housed River Grove Realty.

Then next door to my bakery, Loudon's Antique Emporium, one of the places tourists passing through frequented for furniture, antique jewelry and knickknacks.

Throughout the four blocks, the alley was badly in need of repaving, with cracks in the asphalt and missing chunks. Gravel was strewn across much of the alley. Anyone drunk would have a challenging time navigating the path, especially since it was unlit at night, unless shops had their back lights on.

As I approached the back of The Laughing Loaf, I saw someone moving around near the door. At first, I thought it was Brad Castro going over the crime scene again. As I approached, I saw a large, familiar form step backwards to raise a camera and take pictures. He stepped over the police tape to take photos of the concrete area and the door. I heard the click and whir of the camera.

"Mr. Behrens! You can't be here. The police chief is still examining the scene."

Nate Behrens lowered his camera and stared at me, as if I were the trespasser. "I'm documenting the area where my brother died. He slipped and fell on your back steps. You got a problem with that?"

As I approached, I saw the full length of this man's form in a way I hadn't inside the bakery. He was intimidating—well over six feet and his arms were thick and muscular—like the man on the paper towel package. He stood facing me, looking like a bear, a belligerent one. Where his brother had been thin, lanky, and fine-boned, Nate was massive like a tree trunk. Nate had the same high cheekbones but while Nico's were smooth and sleek, Nate's were cut into his face like ruts carved in stone. His brother belonged on a runway. Nate belonged here in the mountains.

"I understand you are upset, but you can't walk all over a crime site. Who knows what evidence you're contaminating?" I stood my ground. "If you've got problems with the way the case is being handled, talk to Police Chief Westerman."

Nate gave me a dark, cynical look. "A couple of back country cops aren't going to find out who killed my brother. I'll take my own photos." He detached the crime tape and began rotating the lens to take a closeup of the door handle and window.

He couldn't do this. Nate was grieving his loss, but he obviously had little regard for local law enforcement. He also seemed certain that I had simply let his brother fall and die on my back step.

Nate had seemed to grab at this conclusion and held tight. There was nothing I was going to say that would change his mind about me or how this case was being handled.

So I'm not sure why the following words shot out of my mouth.

"I read about your brother and the cuff links."

Nate Behrens's head swung toward me so quickly, it startled me. He let the camera drop and it hung lens down on the strap around his neck.

"What did you read?"

His blue eyes focused hard on me, like sunlight through a magnifying glass. I was a bug under the glass.

Fear percolated in my stomach, but I stood up straight and stared right back at him. "That he was in a photo shoot in Los Angeles with some expensive cufflinks. By the time the shoot was over, they had disappeared."

Nate rubbed his face and took a deep breath. He paused for a while before he spoke, and then his arms relaxed and the tension in his face drained away. He looked out across the alley. I could hear the white noise of the river, rushing over rocks a few yards beyond.

"I brought him here to get away from it." His voice was raspy and thick. "I thought getting him away from LA would stop the spiral he was in. The police couldn't pin anything on him. But everyone assumed he'd done it. He lost out on jobs. Pretty soon he wasn't getting any calls. His agent dropped him. He'd gone from being one of the most in-demand models to—a suspected criminal."

In the light of Nico's recent death, I didn't want to ask the question on my mind. But apparently Nate had been thinking of it.

"I don't know if he did it. Our house was searched, they

found nothing." Nate leaned against the back wall of the bakery. "When I read what happened, it seems obvious. The only one who could have taken those cuff links was Nico. He was the only one who'd been alone with them. He swore to me that he hadn't. He said had no interest in them and wouldn't have jeopardized a career he loved by taking them."

"Was Nico being pursued by anyone up here?" I asked. "Paparazzi? Detectives? Anyone from LA?"

Nate turned his gaze on me, but it was calm now. I wondered how much of my response to him was due to his intensely serious look. He looked like he was grilling me, as if he were perpetually angry.

"I don't think so." He said gruffly as he twisted the large lens off his camera and squatted down to put it away in his bag. "I'm sure someone could have found him up here if they'd been motivated—or paid to find him. But in our time here, he hadn't heard from anyone. Nico said he finally felt safe in River Grove, since people here didn't know him. Nobody was bugging him." He shook his head and the look in his eyes turned to one of great sadness.

I needed to get my loaves and dough going for tomorrow, so I had to excuse myself.

"I'm so sorry about what happened to Nico. I'd talk to the police chief and see what he knows. Dave Westerman isn't a local. He came over from Sacramento, so he's not exactly a backwoods lawman."

Nate blinked at me, his face losing none of its intensity as he thought about this. He frowned. "Yeah. Well, I don't have much of a choice, do I?"

I watched him as he took a final look at the cordoned-off area. Then hoisted his black leather camera bag over one of his massive shoulders and plodded around the corner of the bakery to the main street.

Once inside the bakery, my insides fluttered from my encounter with Nate.

I threw myself into a flurry of activity, mixing the brioche dough, then the cinnamon roll dough, in the stand mixer. I mixed up blueberry scones, rolled them out and did a series of folds to get layers going for laminated dough. Then I cut them into triangles and loaded them onto pans, so I could freeze them and have them ready to bake tomorrow morning.

Just as it had in that year after my mother passed away, the rich smell of the dough comforted me. It was the precursor to warm, baked goodness. All of it comfort food.

With the strange wave of crime that had descended on my new hometown, shaking the place I'd sought refuge, I needed that comfort.

As I was finishing up on the baking table, my phone rang. I dusted as much of the flour off my hands as I could and dug into my purse for it.

"How's the case going, my friend?" It was Elana, and it sounded like she had me on speakerphone in her car. I suspected she'd called because she'd gotten stuck in bumper-to-bumper traffic coming back from San Jose on highway 17 and was bored. "Any news on the man on your back step?"

"Mayor Corinne dropped a hint this morning that the chief thinks Nico Behrens was poisoned." I brushed hair out of my face adding some flour to my cheek in the process. "Which the police chief denied when I asked."

"Hmm, sounds like the police department has a few

leaks." Elana said, as I heard her maps program in the background tell her about an alternate route that could cut five minutes off her trip home. "And Mayor C wants to show everybody she's got the inside scoop."

I felt weird about talking about my interactions with Nate, but I was dying to share it with someone.

"So, Nate Behrens came in yesterday, angry that I didn't hear his brother that night."

"You couldn't have heard what was going on at the back door from the dining area." Elana's voice sounded indignant. "Not with those walls."

"I know, right?" It felt good to have it confirmed by someone else. "Then today, I was coming back from dropping off Biga at home. I went through the alley, and I saw Nate on the back step, taking down the police tape so he could take photos of the door and window."

"What? That's illegal," Elana said, then added as an afterthought, "I mean I assume that's illegal. He shouldn't have done it."

I sighed. "I looked up some info on Nico. He was an underwear model and got in some trouble before he and his brother moved up here. I told Nate that I knew about it."

"Whoa, Gracie— I'm trying to come to terms with the fact that this guy who just moved to River Grove was an *underwear* model." I clearly had her attention. I told her the story I'd read, which Nate had confirmed.

"The police never proved he stole the jewels?"

"Well, no. But everyone thought he did, and it ruined his career. He was a popular model, but he stopped getting gigs. His agent dropped him. Paparazzi followed him. It made his life miserable; that's why Nate convinced him to move up here to get away from everything."

I was starting to relate to Nico Behrens' situation. He

had been a man on the run. He may have done nothing wrong. Like me, maybe he was a victim of a bad set of circumstances.

"I saw the guy's photo in the *Mercury News* this morning." Elana said. "What a hunk. Of course, he was a model. Does the brother look like him?"

"Not at all," I almost muttered it under my breath. I didn't want to talk any more about Nate Behrens. All I could see in my mind was the man's shoulders, those searing eyes and the perpetual scowl on his face.

"Hey, want some company?" Elana perked up. "There's an accident just ahead. I might as well get off 17 at Scott's Valley and take 9. I'll be there in about 15 minutes."

I finished up my loaves, slid them into the proofer and pulled a bottle of emergency zinfandel out of the cabinet above the fridge. I've found it helpful to keep a bottle of red wine ready at all times.

I called my dad to let him know I'd be late for dinner.

I loved my dad. I loved my dog.

But right now, I needed my friend.

Chapter Six

Elana poured more wine into my almost empty glass and let me talk.

"Everyone assumed he stole them. What if someone tracked Nico up here and tried to get the cufflinks from him?" I took a sip of the wine. "Or the money he'd gotten from fencing them?"

"How expensive are we talking?" Elana pulled a bag of vending machine pretzels from her purse, tore the top off and laid the bag on the table for us to share. Definitely not as elegant as our charcuterie the other night, but I was hungry and didn't care. I dumped out a few.

"The article I read said $350,000."

Elana's eyes widened. "They had to be insured. The owner must have gotten a payout. Then that leaves Nico—if he did steal the jewels—with a lot of money. If he can find someone who'd take the risk of buying them."

"Nate said he doesn't think his brother did it." I bit down on a pretzel, which had as much flavor as a dry twig. "Nate said he wouldn't have thrown away a good career by doing something so stupid."

"People don't always want to believe family could commit a crime," Elana leaned back in her chair, her fingers wrapped around her wine glass. "Even when it seems like they obviously did it." She could have a point. Nate was fiercely defensive of Nico. He hadn't mentioned parents or other siblings. Maybe Nico was the only family member he had left.

"In this case, though," I said, tracing the stem of my wine glass with my finger, "it doesn't matter whether Nico stole the cufflinks or not. It's looking impossible for him *not* to have stolen them. Everyone believed did it. He could have been killed for something he didn't even have."

"You should talk to the brother, Gracie." Elana looked at me, then at her watch. "He might know more than he's saying."

I had no desire to talk to Nate Behrens. Why was she pushing me to start nosing around about Nico's death? So I'd read some celebrity gossip. Now I'd gotten sucked into wanting to know why Nico had ended up dead at my doorstep.

My job in River Grove was to run The Laughing Loaf bakery and keep a low profile. I couldn't do this. It was irresponsible—I could risk my father's and my safety.

Looking into the murder of Nico Behrens would *not* keep my visibility low.

* * *

Elana left after downing two glasses of water and some pretzels. I wiped down the baking tables and did a second round through the back room to check on everything. The scones were in the freezer, tubs of cinnamon roll dough were chilling in the fridge. I dumped coffee into the basket of the drip maker and made sure there were coffee cups, paper cups in three sizes and napkins ready at the coffee station. Then I checked the locks on all the doors.

Why I decided to do it right then, I didn't know. I mean, I could have checked the camera footage myself on my computer before I sent it to Police chief Westerman this morning. It had been hard enough thinking about a man meeting his death outside my bakery while I laughed with my friend 150 feet away—I didn't want to watch footage of it. And now, thanks to Nate, guilt nagged me. A cycle of remorse and reassurance revolved in my head as crazily as Biga chasing his tail.

I went into the tiny office next to the baking room, a converted walk-in closet where I kept my computer and printer, did my finances, made orders for supplies, and printed checks. My heart pounded as I turned on the computer.

After inserting the thumb drive into a USB slot in my computer. I took a deep breath as the list of files appeared in a window. I clicked on the file of that night's camera footage

It was a view of the back steps, looking out at the alley during the day. I clicked fast forward and saw a comically sped-up view of the day. Cars pulling in, then whizzing back out of parking spots. People zoomed by: moms with their kids, babies in strollers, an elderly couple in ski jackets hand in hand, toddling side to side in rapidly moving images. I spotted a figure with disheveled red hair and slumped posture, Stewart Hamilton, with coffee in his hand, getting into his car. I saw myself, taking a garbage bag out to the dumpster, then Elana tapping at the back window until I let her in.

As daylight started to fade into night, the busyness stopped. The motion-activated porch light went on and, soon after, a shadow lurched into view. I immediately reached out to slow down the playback. I heard heavy breathing and a moaning noise, guttural almost like an animal.

Nico Behrens stood lit up in the alley, seeming disoriented, as he surveyed his surroundings from side to side. He moved unsteadily on his feet and almost fell. Then he turned around and looked behind him, and his eyes opened wider in fear. He stumbled toward the bakery door. He pounded on the door with his fist and whispered something that sounded like *help*.

He struggled to stay upright, lunging forward and grasping the handle of the door. He pulled it open, then fell hard against the door jamb and slid down, his arm thrust inside.

He lay sprawled in front of the door, as I'd seen him last night.

I stopped the video and rubbed my eyes, which had grown moist. I'd just seen a man die. Nate's accusation that I should have helped his brother came back to me. Nico whispered *help* while I was laughing and drinking wine a few rooms away.

I turned my computer off and sat back in my chair. I remembered Chief Westerman and Brad Castro exchanging glances when they mentioned the video. They'd watched this. What had they seen in this? They had concluded, apparently, that Nico had been poisoned.

This isn't your job, Gracie. You don't have to figure out what happened to Nico Behrens. Feeling guilty because Bear Man thinks you're responsible for his brother's death?

Stop feeling guilty. Nico was deep into a situation that started before he came to River Grove. Your back step didn't kill him, and you couldn't have saved him even if you heard him. And doing something now is a bad idea.

What would the federal marshals say if they knew you were even considering looking into Nico's death on your own?

I grabbed my purse and headed out to my car. I needed a non-pretzel dinner and a good night's sleep.

For all I knew the police chief and his deputy were in the process of solving the case right now.

Chapter Seven

It was 6 a.m. and still dark outside.

Every room in the bakery was lit up, and 8os funk music blared from the speakers, I had two cups of strong coffee in me, and the oven was pumping out smells of sweet, buttery brioche.

I'd come in early with Biga in tow since I couldn't sleep. Biga looked exhausted and skeptical as I coaxed him into the crate, but I could see the wheels turning in his head as he looked at me and settled into the crate. He knew there'd be food in it for him if he went along.

The smells of baking bread did a lot to improve my mood. I knew what I needed to do, and I did it without thinking, sliding pans and baking stones into the oven, taking them out and transporting everything to the cooling racks. It felt comforting to be busy and moving around.

By the time Beck came in the front entrance at 7, I had the blueberry scones in the oven, the last thing I needed to bake this morning. The rich buttermilk smell, along with the scent of fresh baked berries, hung in the air. Even Biga was giving me sad looks, following me with interest. *C'mon —a few crumbs?*

Scenes from the recording still played in my head: Nico's look of fear at something behind him in the alley, and his sudden fall on the step after he opened the back door. I wasn't sure I'd mention what I'd seen on the recording to Beck. I certainly wasn't going to show it to her; it would probably upset her.

Beck walked into the baking room and set down her things on the bottom shelf of the metal table she usually worked at. She seemed unusually subdued this morning.

"Good morning." I gave her a friendly smile. "I used your eggs in the brioche dough. The loaves are smelling amazing."

She turned to look at me, but I still wasn't seeing much of a response. Usually, I could read Beck.

She took her coat off and put on her apron, then pulled up her hair in one of those fountain ponytails that spurt from the top of the heads of women younger than me. She had a worried look on her face.

"Nate Behrens came over last night." Her big brown eyes were wide and slightly red from crying.

"Beck, is everything okay?" I got a sick feeling in the pit of my stomach. I had a feeling that this would not be something I wanted to hear.

She pulled up a stool next to the large center table where I was working.

"Nate thinks that the bakery was at fault in Nico's death. That we—actually *you*, Gracie—sorry—" She looked afraid to tell me this and was embarrassed. "That you should have known Nico was back there. And that Nico's fall on the steps could be what killed him. He said you were *negligent* in maintaining the property." She lowered her eyes, ashamed of saying it.

Negligent. This scared the heck out of me. This could mean a lawsuit, something I couldn't afford. And something that would bring me unwanted attention.

What the heck?

My conversations with Nate Behrens came back to me. Anger took over the lingering guilt I'd felt. If Nico had been poisoned, a fall on the steps hadn't been the cause of his death.

"Beck, do you believe this?"

She swallowed hard. Then she shook her head. "I'm not sure. But he is very angry. He says he's not getting any answers from the police chief, and he's frustrated."

All of the sudden, my anger turned on the police chief. River Grove was supposed to be my safe place to land after going through hell with the ordeal of Ben's confession, arrest, and trial. Now, approaching my one-year anniversary in this town, the peaceful escape I'd found here was quickly dissolving.

I considered the scenario. If Nate was able to get some answers from Police Chief Westerman, he might have some closure and back off. If the case was solved, Nate might drop things completely and move on. I didn't want to deal with Angry Bear, but I might have to talk to him again. His explosive rants to his neighbors might begin to affect the success of The Laughing Loaf, and I wasn't going to let him get away with that. That would have to happen over *my* dead body.

I took a gulp of my quickly cooling coffee then set the coffee mug down a little too hard. It splashed onto the table.

"Thank you for telling me this, Beck. I don't know what

I can do to make him change his mind about this, but it helps to know what he's thinking. He's devastated by Nico's death, and I do feel bad for him."

Beck's eyes teared up. "Me, too. I couldn't handle any of my four brothers dying. My family is so close."

"Let's focus on getting things ready for opening." I turned to pull the blueberry scones out of the oven. "Can you load the display with what we've got on the racks? And check the straws, lids, and napkins. After the morning rush is over, I'm going to track the police chief down and have a talk. You should be fine if I leave around 10."

At 8 a.m., I set the joke of the day on its stand on the counter, thinking of one of Elana's and my common interests.

The Laughing Loaf Joke of the Day
What did the grape say when he was pinched?
Nothing, he just gave a little wine.

There was another line of customers today, and it wound outside the building, bigger than the previous day. Customers looked around, curious, as if the bakery was a carnival sideshow and a cup of coffee was the price of entry. There were moms with their babies. Several of the business owners from up and down the street. Robert Loudon from the Antiques Emporium was in animated conversation with Susan from Cut 'n Curl about an art deco mirror she wanted to sell. A group of teenagers in flannel shirts clumped together at the end of the line—which made me wonder if the high school was having a teacher workday today. Were we somehow a cooler place to hang out because we'd been the scene of a crime?

Jake Daniels was first in line, smelling of fresh Ivory soap, his damp hair slicked back like a middle-aged James Dean. He wore what looked like a bowling shirt with the red and black Speed Spot logo sewn on.

"I'll have a medium latte and a scone, Gracie." He slid his credit card into the pay station and tapped on the screen. "Any news on the murder? I didn't hear about any arrest."

"Me either, Jake." I handed him his scone, which didn't need to be warmed up since it was fresh out of the oven. "Have you heard anything else about the break in?"

Jake frowned. "Not yet. I'm getting a lot of crap from Stewart Hamilton's company, BlueSurf, about the laptop in his car, even though it was obviously his fault for leaving it. But I did have a new security system installed. Cameras, alarms, the whole bit. Anybody tries to break in, they'll go deaf and be recorded by eight different cameras. Expensive as hell, but what can you do?" He shrugged as he went to pick up the latte Beck had just set down at the end of the counter.

Today, I saw someone I don't normally see in the mornings—Reggie McFerrin, manager of The Riverside. Since the music venue didn't close till 2 a.m., Reggie made a habit of sleeping late. The times I did see him in the bakery, he was wearing shades and looking pale and vampire-like.

Reggie was a local celebrity. I noticed customers watching him and whispering amongst themselves.

The man wore a ponytail and had one pierced ear. He had to be in his seventies. Mayor Corinne told me he'd lived in River Grove since the 1960s and had run a commune. He'd started The Riverside in 1980. Over the past 40 years The Riverside had become famous as a small venue for folk, rock, and alternative music acts. People came from all over the Bay Area to see the shows. At least a few of the regulars were bikers, judging by the Harleys parked in front of the saloon.

I remembered the police chief saying that Nico Behrens had been drinking at the saloon the afternoon he'd been killed before he'd made his way down the alley.

If Nico had been poisoned, it could have happened at The Riverside. Not that I was an expert—and it still hadn't been confirmed by anyone that that was his cause of death. But depending on how fast the toxin worked, it could fit the timing of his death, if he'd ended up dead on my back steps around 4:30 p.m.

"Hey, Reggie." I saw my smile reflected in the mirrored lenses of the man's sunglasses. "What brings you in so early this morning?"

"I am in dire need of a latte, Gracie. Can you make that with four shots of espresso?" He pulled a tooled leather wallet out of his jeans pocket that looked old enough to have been unearthed in an archaeological dig. He laid a crumpled ten-dollar bill on the counter. "I've got an early meeting. People don't seem to understand the entertainment business keeps different hours. We don't do the standard 9 to 5."

"Coffee should help, Reggie. We'll have that for you at the end of the counter in just a couple of minutes."

The man gave me a two-finger salute and stepped back to wait for his drink.

Things slowed down around 9:30, though everyone had seemed to want to linger. It had warmed up since yesterday, so the tables outside were filled with customers drinking coffee and gabbing. When I went outside to wipe down tables, I could hear snippets of their conversations. Nico Behrens' death was a major topic. There was a lot of speculation.

"Who ups and moves to a new town like this, when they don't know anybody here?"

"The mafia put a hit out on Nico Behrens."

"I heard the brothers had to leave LA.... Some kind of scandal."

"Murder? I heard the guy died of an overdose."

The tables inside weren't empty. An older couple had opened a game case and were sliding backgammon pieces over a board at a table by the window. The teenagers had taken over one of the large tables and were drinking their sweet, flavored coffees and sharing YouTube videos with each other. It was one of those sights that made me happy to own The Laughing Loaf.

Beck put loaves in the display case, immediately filling the dining area with the aroma of freshly baked brioche and sourdough loaves. The smells were off the charts. My anxiety eating was about to be activated. In the midst of this stress, I wanted to sink my hand into a loaf of buttery sweet brioche, rip off a large hunk and eat it with a latte.

To resist that impulse, I went through the dining area wiping down the vacated tables and filling a plastic bin with used mugs and plates to take back to my super-fast commercial dishwasher.

At 10 a.m., I waved at Beck and went out the front door in search of the police chief. My first stop—the most likely place to find him at this hour - was at his desk at River Grove City Hall, which was in the remodeled old River Grove General Hardware building across the street. Mayor Corinne had her office there and there was a room the police chief and his deputy used for making calls and receiving guests.

I opened the old, green-painted front door and stepped into the small lobby, where I saw a young woman, sporting a highly placed fountain of hair like Beck's, sitting at a computer desk, typing away. The place had the delicious smell of old wood, new paint and fresh coffee and scones— from my bakery.

I suspected this was the young intern Mayor C had mentioned hiring this month. A homemade name plate on her desk said PEONY ROBERTS.

"How may I help you, ma'am?" The young woman looked me over, taking inventory.

Seriously—ma'am? Ma'ams were at least fifty, and I had more than fifteen years before that form of address would apply to me.

"Gracie Markley, from The Laughing Loaf." I said, curtly, as I looked down the hall in the direction of the room I was interested in. "I'm here to talk to the police chief. Is he in?" I heard Chief Westerman's voice echoing down the hall. I knew he was.

She rose from her seat. "Let me check—"

"I'll save you the trouble and head back there myself, Peony. Thank you." As she started to look huffy, I flashed her a smile and made my way down the hall, past framed historical photos of River Grove over the years.

There were photos of the old log flume, which had been used to transport logs from the lumber operations in the mountains down to a mill at the outskirts of town. Redwood lumber from the logging operations was used to build houses and structures all over Northern California and then supplied the wood to rebuild those destroyed in the 1906 San Francisco Earthquake and fire.

I saw a photo of the building that now stood next to my bakery: Loudon's Emporium, originally a general store, run by Robert Loudon's great grandfather. And an old photo of my bakery building from 1915, with its original owner in a suit and comically large moustache, standing proudly in front of his bank, which catered to the loggers. A warm feeling came over me as I recognized the bones of the building that I'd come to love. I felt grounded somehow, grafted into the history of this town.

Dave Westerman was talking to someone on the phone, as he leaned back in his chair at a precipitous angle, the way teachers warned students not to do in middle school. The police chief was a heavy-set man, who looked like he did more sitting than chasing bad guys.

He looked up at me, startled. He didn't look happy to see me as he continued talking on the phone.

"I'll call you back, Rick. But the sooner you get me those test results, the better."

He pressed the button to end the call and replaced the receiver. With a *thunk*, the chair tipped forward and all six legs concerned were on the floor.

"Good morning, Dave."

"What brings you in to see me, Gracie? Isn't this your busy time over at The Laughing Loaf?" He frowned as he got up and pulled an old captain's chair from the corner and set it down in front of his desk for me.

I sat down.

"I need to talk to you about your investigation into Nico Behrens' death the other day."

"Now, Gracie." He held up his hands in *whoa* position, as if ready to fend me off. "This is really not your—"

"For one thing, how long are you going to be blocking off my back step?" I tried to make myself comfortable in the old captain's chair. "We're receiving all our deliveries through the front. It's an inconvenience to go through the front for everything, especially during business hours. Delivery trucks are blocking traffic."

"We'll take down the tape this afternoon." Westerman nodded. "I just talked to Brad. Crime scene's given us all we're gonna get."

I hadn't expected it to be so easy. "Thank you." I launched into my next point. "And I have to tell you that Nate Behrens has been accusing me of negligence in the death of his brother. I think he's frustrated. His brother's dead, and he says he's not getting any answers from you. I thought that if he sat down and talked to you—"

The police chief's face twisted into a patronizing smile.

"But you two ladies were drinking now, weren't you?" He sat back in his chair, looking smug. "Maybe you were a little tipsy and gabbing too loud to hear what was going on in the back. Have you thought about that?"

What the heck. I pressed my lips together tightly to keep the angry words from spilling out.

"Dave, I have a business to run. I can't afford to get *tipsy.* And if I did, one glass of wine wouldn't do it." I took a breath. I would not let this man get to me. I also didn't want to alienate him by getting angry right now. I needed his help. I kept my voice steady and cool.

"I did see the footage from my cameras. Nico was staggering down the alley. He seemed disoriented." I watched his eyes. "Was he poisoned?"

The police chief frowned and became suddenly interested in shuffling the paperwork on his desk.

He took a drink from his Laughing Loaf latte—a latte he seemed to be enjoying. From *my* bakery. "We're waiting for the toxicology report. We're not sure where this happened, or when. When we find out the poison and the amount in his system, we'll have a better idea of when it happened."

I sat up in the uncomfortable chair, hoping better posture would help.

"On the footage, I could see Nico approaching, coming down the alley. He must have come from The Riverside. I heard he was seen there. He could have met up with someone there who poisoned him—"

The police chief suddenly widened his eyes, as if I'd said something offensive. "Be careful now, Gracie. The Riverside has been an institution in this town for fifty years. Reggie McFerrin has served four terms as mayor."

"I'm not accusing Reggie of anything, Chief. I'm just saying Nico Behrens was seen drinking there. Nico was coming down the alley from that direction and it was pretty clear from the footage that he was stumbling, gasping for air. He was not well."

"We've looked at the footage." Westerman nodded quickly, impatient. "We've talked to Reggie McFerrin. He says the bartender served Mr. Behrens two drinks that afternoon and that the man sat in a booth by himself. Mr. Behrens complained to the waitress that his drink wasn't made right. His behavior escalated, and he got in an altercation with another customer who Mr. Behrens thought was insulting him. The bartender didn't want a fight, so he kicked him out."

I wondered if Westerman knew about Nico's past. He probably didn't frequent celebrity gossip sites as often as I did. He was more of a *Field and Stream* kind of guy.

"Dave, Nico was in some trouble in Los Angeles before he and his brother moved up here. Do you know anything about that?" I wondered if the news hadn't gone out on any police reports because, while Nico had been suspected of stealing the cufflinks, he'd never been arrested.

The police chief crossed his arms and leaned back in his chair. He looked skeptical but curious at the same time.

"What kind of trouble?"

I told him what I'd read—and that Nate had confirmed it to me. I looked up a story on my phone and passed it on to the police chief, who picked up the phone and began reading.

A MODEL HEIST: *How Supermodel Nico Behrens Pulled Off the Crime of the Century*

Nico Behrens: Diamond in the "Buff"?

"Nate told me he'd moved his brother up here hoping to get away from the bad press. The harassment from the paparazzi was making his life miserable. Everyone seemed sure that he'd taken the cufflinks. What if someone tracked him down in River Grove and wanted those cufflinks back? Or any money he'd received from selling them?"

Police Chief Westerman didn't look very enthusiastic about the information I was passing his way.

"I'll talk to my contacts in Los Angeles and see what I can find out." He said gruffly, taking another sip of his Laughing Loaf latte and smacking his lips. "I suppose it could be worth talking to Nate Behrens to hear more about the theft."

I was beginning to think my mission had been accomplished. My back step would be free of police tape by this afternoon, and I could once again go in my bakery's back entrance. And Chief Westerman would be talking to Nate Behrens—something that needed to happen.

I wouldn't have to worry about Nate Behrens, and his insinuations that I was responsible for his brother's death.

Something told me it wasn't going to be that easy.

And, of course, it wasn't.

Chapter Eight

As I headed back to The Laughing Loaf, I got a text from Beck saying Biga was in watchdog mode and was barking at everyone who walked in the door. I groaned and sped up.

As I approached the bakery, I saw Nate Behrens walking out. He was wearing his mountain man uniform today: khaki hiking pants with zip-off leg panels. Sturdy canvas boots made for hiking rugged terrain. He was armed with his camera—and a large coffee.

I didn't feel like talking to the guy right now. I considered my options. Dart into Loudon's Antique Emporium? Hide my face and walk toward the bakery, pretending I didn't see him?

None of my options were good, so I decided to meet the challenge head on.

"Good morning, Nate." I nodded and smiled, though I wasn't feeling it. "I see you've got your coffee."

He looked up at me, startled. Maybe he hadn't wanted to see me just as much as I hadn't wanted to see him. He gave me a bleary look and searched my face for a moment. I had to remember: this guy thought I was responsible for his brother's death.

"I'm on my way down to Santa Cruz. There's a heron's nest I need to photograph. Near Natural Bridges." He looked a little confused. He looked across the street at city hall, where I had just come from. "Then two minutes ago I got a call from the police chief that he wants to talk to me about Nico's case."

That was fast. Westerman called him right after I'd left. I patted myself on the back for setting that up.

"I hope he gets you some answers, Nate. And again, I'm very sorry for your loss."

The man's face softened just a bit. He nodded at me, his lips opening as if he was going to say something. Good. Maybe everything would be just fine. A man who was into nature photography couldn't be bad, could he? He was probably a nice guy. I hoped the police chief found the person responsible for his brother's death—and soon.

He nodded. "If his death had to do with the cufflinks, I want to know. Maybe this wasn't the safe place I thought it was for him. That girl—who lives down the road from us, she told me—"

"Rebecca, who works with me—Beck?"

He rubbed his face. "Yeah. She grew up here. She said things like that don't happen here. Have never happened here."

I could empathize. Maybe no place was free from crime. Even River Grove, the town where the federal marshals had insisted "nothing ever happened."

"I didn't think so either, Nate. But there are some great things about this town, despite the recent crime surge. Most of the people here are friendly and kind. They've got each other's backs. When someone's down on their luck here, people pitch in, whether that's a drive for funds or a benefit show at The Riverside. I hope you're here long enough to see the good side of River Grove."

Where the hell did that come from, Gracie? Who made you River Grove's goodwill ambassador?

I had no idea what had prompted this sudden surge of town fervor. Part of me hoped that Nate Behrens would stay and see that this place was full of good people. Who like they had done for me, would accept him into the fold and make him feel welcome.

Nate looked at me, dazed. This time, no searing gaze with those laser blue eyes. I don't know if what I'd said even registered with him.

He grunted and looked again across the street.

"Yeah. Well, I should go talk to the chief."

He looked both ways, then lumbered across the small downtown street toward city hall.

When I got back to the bakery, we were experiencing a sudden wave of customers asking for "whatever the bread is that's smelling so good outside." Beck gave me a panicked look as she nodded toward the growing line of customers who wanted brioche.

Robert Loudon, of Loudon's Antique Emporium, stood waiting for his coffee—and not very patiently.

"Seems like you're getting all the business these days, Gracie." He frowned as he looked around the dining area. "You care to share any of that with me?"

I'd heard Loudon's Antiques had been losing business over the past year, but I hardly thought I was taking any away from him. It's not like people strolled by and said: *Hmm, bread or an armoire today? Which will it be?*

I went to the back room and took all the loaves from the cooling racks, loaded them into paper sleeves and filled a basket with them. I'd have to consider putting brioche in our regular rotation.

I opened up a second line and began taking customers. We had to tell the last customer in line we were out, but I was able to convince them that the country sourdough today was also very good.

After fifteen minutes, everyone had left the counter, and a couple of customers had taken their coffee drinks to the dining area.

"I had no idea that would happen. We usually have a slow period at ten,"

I told her as she made herself an iced coffee and prepared to sit down for a break. "What's the deal with Robert Loudon today? He seems angry that we're busy and he's not."

"His mother died a few months ago. Cancer." Beck said sadly. "I feel bad for him. She was in charge of buying the store's antiques, and I think he's having a hard time without her."

Of course. I felt bad for not remembering the woman had died. I'd met Iris Loudon last year. She'd given me a River Grove history lesson and showed me old photos of the mountain logging camps, built on rail cars—called Rollervilles—so they could be moved as the forest receded.

I found my almost-cold coffee and followed Beck back to the baking room, taking a seat across from her on one of the stools. She looked down at the table, her smooth forehead wrinkling into a frown.

"Why does it seem like we're getting more business now than ever?" She took a sip of her iced drink. "After Nico's death, I mean."

From the longer lines at opening and the unexpected

business later in the day, it did seem like more people were coming into The Laughing Loaf.

I grabbed a metal scraper and worked at cleaning globs of dough off the bread table.

"It could be that people are curious." I swept the debris of the table into a pile and then swept it into the trash. "But maybe this is their way of coming together in a hard time. We both know that baked goods comfort people. We've had some scary things happen in town. Maybe that makes them want to gather together and talk about it, and this is where they choose to do it. It's bad that Nico died here, but maybe it's good that everyone's meeting here."

Beck set her drink down on the table, her brown eyes thoughtful. "I didn't think of it that way, Gracie. People come to The Laughing Loaf as a way to deal with what's been going on."

And hopefully, right now, Nate Behrens was asking his questions and finding out about his brother's case.

"Nate's with Chief Westerman." I said, as I grabbed a misshapen blueberry scone from today's discard pile. My lunch.

Biga gave me a pleading look, so I broke off a small corner and he put his paws on the gate, and I let him gobble it from my hand. "I hope he gets reassurance that the Chief and Deputy Castro are working to find Nico's killer."

I hoped the killer would be found, and soon. But one thing scared me. Mayor Corinne was sure that all these things were the work of outsiders coming into our town to cause trouble.

What if the killer was one of us?

* * *

I decided to keep Biga at the bakery for the rest of the day. But I did need to take him out for a walk, and I could do with some fresh air myself.

At 11:30 a.m., when I was fairly sure the bakery wouldn't be overwhelmed by a sudden surge in business, I left Beck in charge and took Biga on a walk. We followed the alley down past the last business on the main street, then followed a trail through the woods until we came to the river.

Biga couldn't believe his good luck. He trotted ahead of me, pulling on the leash, and sniffing every tree and bush. He did his business more times than I thought possible.

The air along the river was cool, thick with the rich smell of redwoods and aromatic laurel. On this cloudy day, the canopy overhead kept things so dark, it looked like it was nearing dusk. I shivered and wished I'd brought a heavier jacket. There was a stillness here, as if the canopy above me and the huge trees around me were dampening all sound.

My thoughts drifted back to hikes I'd taken with Ben on our many trips together. Hikes through tropical rain forests in South America, backpacking in the Swiss Alps. A trek up to a temple in the mountains of China. We'd loved exploring new places, the more far-flung the better. He used to tell me I was the only person he could imagine sharing these adventures with. Yet my fond memories of these trips were ruined when I found out that he was not the man I thought I'd married. Over the past year, I saw how many red flags I'd missed because I hadn't wanted to see them. I vowed to myself I would never make that mistake again.

Biga and I walked past the edge of downtown, so I looked around to figure out where we were now. We were no longer within civilization it seemed. The river was widening as it headed eagerly for the ocean, tumbling impatiently over the rocks in its way. The redwoods seemed bigger here, massive trunks that would take a few people joined together to wrap their arms around. I saw a sight I'd learned to get used to: a bright yellow banana slug near a tree moving imperceptibly slowly. They were slimy and alien-looking with their tiny antennae.

The banana slug was the mascot of nearby University of California at Santa Cruz, where they were looked upon affectionately. I didn't feel the same way about the slimy creatures. It's possible that more time in the area would help me with that, but I wasn't holding out hope.

I waited for Biga to finish his business next to a bush, then started heading back toward town. We retraced our steps along the river. There was a bounce in Biga's step; I hadn't taken him on a long walk in a while, not like we used to before we moved here. Despite the judgy looks he'd given me lately at the bakery, he immediately forgave me today for not paying attention to him, because that's what dogs do. Another characteristic that makes dogs superior to humans, in my opinion.

As we neared the edge of town, about fifty feet from Speed Spot Motors, a figure moved beyond a stand of trees. I heard the scrape of a shovel against dirt and rocks. I sped up to see where it was coming from. Behind a line of shrubs, I saw someone shoveling dirt over something, then stamping on the ground. When the person was done, they headed toward the stairs of The Riverside, shovel in hand.

When he turned on the steps to look back at the spot, the sun glinted off the mirrored shades of Reggie McFerrin.

* * *

Beck was in front, finishing off an espresso drink for a customer when I came in the front door of The Laughing Loaf with Biga. My mind was spinning with questions about what Reggie McFerrin had been doing in the woods. And how Nate's conversation with the police chief had gone.

Beck smiled at me as she pulled the oat milk out of the mini fridge. I immediately looked over to see Mayor Corinne waiting at the counter for her drink in her yellow fireplug jacket. Beck was working on two drinks, so I assumed the mayor was taking one back for the chief.

"Good to see you, Mayor C." I smiled and went to put Biga behind his gate and refill his water bowl. The dog began lapping furiously. After washing my hands, I went out front to chat.

Beck had just put down a second drink at the pickup area and handed Mayor C a drink carrier.

"How are things, Corinne?" I asked as casually as I could, as I glanced at the display case. Beck had already restocked.

Mayor C let out a sigh as she fit the drinks into the carrier. "As good as can be expected, I guess. I've called a community meeting for tomorrow morning down in the River Grove High School theatre—don't know if you heard. Chief Westerman and I want to discuss the progress on the current crime cases and put a call out for tips. We've decided to offer a reward for information."

I was glad to hear the mayor was taking action. Some pretty wild rumors had been circulating in the dining area about Nico's murder. This meeting could be an opportunity to communicate clearly and maybe draw out anybody who'd seen Nico that night.

"That's smart, Mayor C. It's been two days, and I can tell people are getting uneasy."

I wondered if the police chief had talked about the cuff-link case with Nate—and possibly gotten some background information from him.

Mayor C looked up at me as she balanced her drinks carrier.

"And one more thing. I'd like to order ten trays of cinnamon rolls and two coffee carriers for tomorrow, Gracie."

I shot a look at Beck, who nodded. "I think we can handle that," I said. "We'll bring them over to the high school."

I'd start a double batch of dough this afternoon before I left for the day.

"I ran into Nate Behrens earlier." I dropped in brightly. "He was on his way to talk to the chief."

Mayor C gave me a suspicious look, as if to say, *what's it to you?*

"Nate had told me he was frustrated because he wasn't getting any information on the case," I clarified.

Mayor C nodded, as her lips turned up in a knowing smile. "Yes, it turned out to be a *very* good thing for them to talk this morning. The police chief said it benefitted them both."

What was it about Mayor C that she had to drop these hints? I chalked it up to the woman wanting to remind everyone in town she was in the loop.

Hopefully Nate had given the police chief some background information on his brother. And the police chief had updated Nate on the progress of the investigation. I had to keep reminding myself that this was none of my business. The tape was coming down on the back entrance. I had more customers than ever right now, so much that if these surges continued, I'd need to bring Beck on for more hours.

"Glad to hear it, Mayor C." I was in a good mood now, though the strange image of Reggie McFerrin burying something in the woods kept intruding on my thoughts. "Can I get you and the police chief some blueberry scones? It's on the house."

Mayor C looked up with interest. "Yes, Gracie. We'd love that."

I grabbed two of the blueberry scones and put them in a bag, then handed them over the counter to her. She nodded her thanks and perched the bag between the two drinks on her drink carrier. I went around the counter to open the front door for the mayor, and she headed out, making her way across the street.

Then I asked Beck if she could come in earlier tomorrow morning to work on the mayor's order.

"No problem, Gracie. It should be slower here, too. Most of our customers will be at the meeting."

"I was going to ask you to deliver it, but I think I should go."

Beck's face grew serious. She looked down at the table. "They'll be talking about the murder. Of course, you need to go, Gracie. I can handle things here. You need to find out what's going on. If any more information has been released about Ni—. I mean, I want to know."

I wondered if Nate Behrens would be there. If he was, I hoped he wouldn't publicly point an accusing finger at me. If he did, at least I'd be there to defend myself.

I nodded. "Beck, you're right. I do need to be there. Thanks for being flexible. Kind of an exciting, isn't it? Our first catering gig."

Her eyes brightened suddenly.

"Hey, did you see the foam art I did on the mayor's drink? Of course, oat milk is harder to work with than regular milk. But I'm working hard on my laughing loaf image. A loaf of bread with a big smile."

Beck had been improving her skills at making designs in the crema for the lattes and cappuccinos. She was doing hearts now, and they were precise and recognizable. She had tried to do a unicorn, but it ended up looking like a misshapen goat.

"We've got some down time now. I could use a latte. Try doing the loaf image on it. I'd love to see what you've been working on."

"Of course, Gracie!"

I went back into the baking room to mix another batch of scones, since we still had blueberries left.

I could hear Beck at work on the machine, preparing the drink. In a couple minutes, she brought back a drink and laid it down on the metal worktable before me then stepped back with a look of excited expectation.

I looked down to see a mug with a foamy, floating image in it. It looked like a tin can with wings. I could sort of see the outline of a bread loaf. But the loaf wasn't laughing. It was leering at me.

"I think you're getting the idea, Beck." I smiled, trying to find the line between honesty and encouragement. "What do you think of it?"

"I'm getting better. I need to practice more, though." She turned up the corner of her mouth. "Oh, and I forgot to tell you. While you were out, you got a letter. It came special delivery. It looks really official."

"Who's it from?"

"Somebody here in town. Peter James Jordan, Attorney at Law."

Chapter Nine

I went home that evening, after prepping dough for loaves and sliding two trays of scones into the freezer for tomorrow.

My head was buzzing with anxious thoughts about Nate taking legal action. I told myself I'd put off opening the attorney's letter until I got home and had a snifter of brandy in my hand. My dad was happy to join me in having some brandy before dinner.

Biga seemed to pick up on my distress. He curled up next to me on the sofa and rubbed his head up against my legs.

"No update on the murder case?" My dad asked once he'd taken a few sips of brandy. "I haven't heard much about it in the news."

"I did tell the police chief he needed to talk to Nate Behrens about his brother's past," I said, as the brandy began to calm my buzzing brain. I told him briefly about Nico and the jewels. And Nate's photography session on my back step. "Nate met with the police chief this morning.

I hope Westerman convinced him that they are working hard on the case."

I didn't want to worry my father, so I didn't bring up the letter from the attorney. I'd wait till I knew more before I talked to him about any legal action.

I wanted to talk to Elana, though. I'd text her tonight.

"It sounds like this could be related to Nico's theft—or non-theft—of the jewels," my dad said as he swirled the last of his brandy in its glass. Biga looked up at the glass, realized it wasn't food, then put his head back down on my father's leg to sleep. "Someone wanted to track him down and find out where he'd hidden the cufflinks. What an odd thing—I didn't think anyone even wore cufflinks these days, except posh toffs."

I laughed, imagining Nico Behrens and mountain man Nate Behrens as "posh toffs"—fancy elegant men. This woke Biga up. He looked around and growled suspiciously.

After we ate my father's favorite informal dinner of Welsh rarebit and tomato soup, I left my father to his biography of Nikola Tesla. I went back to my bedroom, letter in hand.

The Welsh rarebit had been delicious, dollops of mustardy, ale-infused melted cheddar on Laughing Loaf sourdough. Now it was churning in my stomach in a sea of tomato soup as I stared down at the envelope.

Open the damn thing, Gracie. It does no good to put these things off. You've been through enough legal trouble to know this.

As I stared at it, I thought of Nate, angry at his brother's death, searching for anything or anyone to blame.

I slit open the letter. From the number of INSERT NAME blanks, it looked like this was a template he used frequently.

. . .

Gracie Lauren Markley
Owner
<u>THE LAUGHING LOAF BAKERY</u>

This is to inform you that you and your establishment <u>The Laughing Loaf Bakery</u> are under investigation for negligence in the death of Nicholas Anthony Behrens, who slipped and fell on the steps of your back entrance on the evening of February 15.

You will be asked to give testimony concerning your knowledge of this event and submit to a search of <u>The Laughing Loaf Bakery</u> property by investigators. Note that it will be to your advantage to cooperate with this investigation.

Questions on this matter may be directed to my assistant Janine Carothers or myself.

Regards,
Peter James Jordan
Attorney at Law

I read the letter twice. I considered calling the marshals assigned to me in WITSEC—my handlers, so to speak. From what I'd heard, they were used to dealing with legal matters for their clients, since many of them were criminals given an opportunity to turn over a new leaf after giving testimony. Compared to what they usually dealt with, my situation didn't seem that bad: a man had fallen on my back porch, and I hadn't heard him call for help. I hadn't offed any informers or staged any heists.

But if this was anywhere near going to court—or would go public in the media, they needed to know. I would rather not have it get to that stage.

I texted Elana. I led with what I'd seen on my walk today. Telling her about the attorney's letter would have made it more real. I was still in denial.

> I saw something weird near the river today.
> If you've got a minute, give me a call.

I clocked it. She called thirty seconds after I hit send.

I told Elana about Reggie McFerrin digging by the river.

"He looked around, trying to make sure no one saw him. I don't think he spotted me."

"What could he be burying? The poison used to kill Nico?"

"Maybe. Or something that might incriminate him." I tried to remember if I'd seen any hint of what he was putting in the hole. I'd been too far away to see.

"Nico was drinking at The Riverside that afternoon. Reggie or someone else at the saloon could have done it."

"Yeah, but why?" Elana asked. "Nico might have been a rowdy customer, but Reggie's run The Riverside for over forty years. I'm sure he's had his share of drunk customers and he hasn't killed anyone yet." She paused and let out a nervous laugh. "As far as I *know*."

I remembered Reggie McFerrin's waxy, vampire-like skin and his eyes hidden behind his sunglasses. Maybe he was a local legend. A former mayor of River Grove, as chief

Westerman had said. Near the river, he'd looked like someone with something to hide. But was the chief willing to question McFerrin about the murder? Would he actually press him for answers? From what the chief had said this morning, he considered McFerrin above reproach.

"Chief Westerman seemed to think there's no way McFerrin could be involved. But if Nico was poisoned, there's a good chance it happened at The Riverside."

"It's not like Reggie himself had to have done it, either. He could have suspected it happened at his saloon. He's got a business to run, just like you do," Elana said. "He could be trying to protect it."

She made a good point, though I'd been hoping for a little more sympathy from my friend. Still, she didn't know my new identity and my need to stay out of the spotlight.

Then Elana surprised me.

"Do you remember the spot where he buried it? Could you find it again?"

"I think I could."

"Then let's go find it and do some digging," Elana said with excitement in her voice. "Let's see what he buried. I mean, why not?"

Now I had to tell her about the attorney's letter. I had to tell someone, even if I didn't want to.

"There's something else. I received a letter from an attorney here in town." I told her about the letter from Peter James Jordan.

"Wow." Elana took a deep breath. "Nate went ahead with it."

"It sounds like he's blaming Nico's death on his slipping on the steps on the bakery. That they weren't well kept up and Nico slipped and fell, which contributed to his death." As I said it, I felt a new pang of sympathy for Nate Behrens.

From his perspective, my property had caused his brother to fall and then die. But if he'd been poisoned, the fall had been the result of his poisoning.

"If he's been poisoned, the suit will be thrown out," Elana said confidently. "Nate Behrens is spending a lot of money to vent his anger."

"I don't think there's any truth to it, but I don't want to go through the investigation. I just want to bake bread and make good coffee for my town. Customers have been great so far—we've had more people coming in this week than ever. But news of a negligence suit? That does not make us look good."

"Hon, if you need an attorney, I can give you the name of a good one."

"Thanks, Elana. I appreciate that. I just want this stopped."

I couldn't tell her about my past. About the ordeal of testifying against Ben and having to create an entirely new life for my dad and me in River Grove.

I was being nudged into a difficult choice; one I'd been avoiding.

"But what can you do about it?" She asked. "Aside from lawyering up?"

It was becoming clear to me. To keep me and The Laughing Loaf out of trouble, I'd need to be proactive. For the first time, I said it out loud.

"I'm going to figure out who killed Nico Behrens."

Chapter Ten

T he next morning was the mayor's town meeting at River Grove High School—and The Laughing Loaf's first catering gig.

I'd need to put aside my worries about Nate's lawsuit and get to work. Beck and I both came in early. We had to produce cinnamon rolls and coffee in Cambros for about two hundred and fifty people and transport it all to the high school.

Beck would stay behind to keep an eye on Biga and man The Laughing Loaf, though I didn't expect many customers at the bakery this morning.

I'd come in feeling more settled. After we'd both had our first cups of coffee, Beck and I were energized to start the day. We had a mission.

With her hair in braids, Beck looked like young Judy Garland in *The Wizard of Oz* as she pulled out large Cambros for coffee and set them aside, then packed containers with cups, lids and stirrers. She was in a better mood today.

After the disturbing letter, I wanted to plunge myself

into the regular routine, throw myself into the ebbs and flows of a day of baking and feeding people. I willed myself to get back to the joy of this business I'd started—which had been interrupted by Nico's death.

"Can you mix the cinnamon filling?" I called out to her as she hung up her coat. "I'll have the dough rolled out in about fifteen minutes."

"On it!" Beck called out as she melted butter in our biggest pot on the stove, then added the premixed proportions of brown sugar and cinnamon—and dollops of my secret ingredient, caramel ice cream topping. A comforting smell filled the bakery. We both sang at the top of our lungs to Duran Duran and A-ha. We must not have been very good, because during "Hungry Like the Wolf," Biga began whimpering, as if he was begging us to stop.

Beck bent down in front of his gate and cocked her head.

"We're that bad, Biga?"

"Or he smells the cinnamon rolls and doesn't understand why he's not getting any." My dog was now on his back legs, pressing his front paws up against the gate. I went over to the cabinet and pulled out his treat bag. His head followed me all the way.

"I know it's driving you crazy, Biga. You've been very patient," I said, as I held up a treat. "Good boy. Here you go." He took the treat from my hand.

I washed my hands carefully and dried them on a towel.

Beck and I worked nonstop till the store opened, making sure everything was ready for the community meeting and our regular customers. By 8:30, the big brown, to-go coffee Cambros were ready to be filled, and multiple batches of cinnamon rolls were baking in my multi-tray oven.

I set out the joke of the day on its stand, one of my favorites.

The Laughing Loaf Joke of the Day
I never wanted to believe that my dad was stealing from his job as a road worker. But when I got home, all the signs were there.

We opened The Laughing Loaf to a much shorter line than usual. Jake from Speed Spot was first in line. followed by Chief Westerman.

"Sure, I'm going to the meeting," Jake said, as he slid his debit card into the pay station. "I'm going to talk about our new security system. I want to hear what the mayor and police chief are planning to do about the crime wave here. I want to know why it's been three days and I still have no answers about the thefts on my lot."

I couldn't tell if Jake Daniels didn't know the police chief was in line right behind him or if he'd made the comment as a purposeful dig.

"Jake, I'm right here." The chief sighed heavily and gave the mechanic a weary look. "We are working on the case. If you have questions, you need to come talk to me instead of making comments in public—"

Jake stepped over to the end of the counter to pick up his drink where Beck had just set it down. "Dave, I get that a murder takes precedence over a burglary, but I've been running Speed Spot in River Grove for twenty years. My dad ran it for twenty-five years before me. The thefts make us look bad. When you showed up to make out the report all you did was lecture me on my security system. I need your support, man. And some answers. You need to figure out who did this."

Jake's voice got louder as he went on. The chief's face turned beet red as he looked like he was preparing his reply. Customers in line watched this with interest—and maybe a little fear.

I stepped out from behind the counter, where I'd been filling the case with fresh cinnamon rolls and scones.

"Chief and Jake, take this outside please." I steered the two men toward the door. "Dave, I'll bring out your latte. It'll be up in just a minute." Glaring at each other, Jake and Dave headed out the front door to the outside seating area.

I met Beck's look of worry and sighed. I hoped this wasn't an indication of how this morning's meeting at the high school would go. The tension in River Grove was high. I hated that my town was on edge. The friendly, supportive little community that I had come to love had become a place of uncertainty and fear.

While Beck handled the small line of customers, I filled the coffee dispensers from the large drip maker in the back room. Ten trays of cinnamon rolls were wrapped and ready. I went out the back to my Subaru parked in the alley and began loading everything into the hatch.

Once I got into my car, the concentrated scents of cinnamon, butter and coffee helped soothe my anxiety about the meeting. A little aromatherapy was never a bad thing. I would swing by the house to pick up my dad, who was interested in attending the meeting. He would be my moral support today, especially if Nate Behrens would be there, too. I didn't want to see the man. I didn't want to talk to him, see those light blue eyes glaring at me. I only wanted to hear what the mayor and the police chief had to say about the recent crimes. Who knew, maybe Mayor C's hints were an indication that the chief had some news about Nico's murder.

If I was to move behind the scenes in trying to solve this case, I needed all the information I could get.

When I got to our house, my father was standing on the front steps, dressed in his tweed jacket and slacks, a brown bow tie at his throat—his professor uniform. His thinning grey hair was slicked down. He'd put serious time into this look. I stifled a laugh.

"You look great, Dad," I said as he opened the door and slid into the passenger seat. "Just a thought here—you might be a little overdressed for this."

"I've never been to one of these meetings, so I erred on the side of dressing my best." He looked over at me as he clicked his seatbelt in place.

"Dad, you're going to make me look bad." I brushed flour off my blue striped button-down shirt. I'd taken off my Laughing Loaf apron, but besides that, I was wearing the jeans I'd put on at 5:30 this morning. I glanced in the rear-view mirror to check my reflection. My hair looked decent, my cheeks looked rosy from the warmth of the kitchen and the cold outside. "I don't know what to expect either. I just hope we get some information on the chief's progress on Nico's case."

"Statistically, this crime wave has to be an anomaly," My father said as we headed down Main Street toward the turn off for the high school. "I don't know why people are afraid. There hasn't been a murder in River Grove since 1982. I googled it. And River Grove is rated one of the safest places to live in Santa Cruz County." My father lived in a world of calculated probabilities, equations, and empirical data. He trusted in these things more than he trusted in people, which from our experience, I could kind of understand.

"Dad, when something like this happens, people immediately think of how it's going to affect *them*. They don't think in terms of statistics or probability."

"But you see, they *shouldn't*. It's much more likely for a mishap to come from another external cause—an earthquake, for example, or a fire. There is precedence for those happening regularly in River Grove."

He was right. We were on the west side of the infamous San Andreas Fault in River Grove. And wildfires happened nearly every year in dry, rain-starved Northern California—especially in the Santa Cruz mountains.

"But people can prepare for those things at least somewhat, dad." I pulled into the entrance to River Grove High School and headed for the back theatre entrance, where I could park and unload. "With a murder, you're dealing with the unpredictable mind of a human being. The killing could be random. People don't know why Nico was killed, or who killed him, so they don't know if it could happen to them—or their children."

I could feel my father staring at me, as I hit the remote to open the back hatch of the car. I turned to him. He had that look he got when I was a kid and he'd asked me to do a math problem in my head.

"Do you think the killing of Nico Behrens was random, dear?"

And of course, I knew the answer to that question.

I watched as Mayor C and the chief headed into the theatre. I remembered Nico stumbling down the alley, a dazed look in his eyes—looking with fear at someone in front of him.

"No, Dad. I don't believe it was random."

* * *

Robert Loudon and Jake Daniels saw us get out of the car and hurried our way to help carry the coffee Cambros into the theater.

A group of students had just finished setting up a long table in the lobby of the small theatre. I covered it with a white linen tablecloth I'd brought from home. Dad and I began setting up the coffee service and trays of rolls.

As my dad stood behind the table, he was getting looks from some of the older ladies coming into the meeting. I'm sure he was taking their attention as validation of his wardrobe choice.

"Dad, go ahead." I waved him toward the auditorium doors.

"I thought you needed my help," he said as he looked at the people coming in.

"I've got this. Save us seats near the front." I smiled at him.

Soon the community of River Grove began pouring in, a half hour before the meeting was to begin. This was the biggest thing to happen in town since I'd lived here. Nearly everyone stopped to talk, get coffee, and grab a cinnamon roll. A gentle roar of conversation filled the lobby.

People who hadn't seen each other in a while stood off to the side to chat. With the coffee and rolls as a draw, I got to see many new faces.

"I want to thank you for that brioche, hon." An older woman in a red Forty-Niners sweatshirt and jeans came up to me. "My husband Jake brought it home last night and it was fantastic."

"You must be Jeanne Daniels." I handed her a cup of coffee and laughed. "You're welcome. He was lucky he came in when he did."

An older couple, the Mortons, who'd been stopping by

The Laughing Loaf with their dog most mornings came over to fill up their coffee mugs.

"Hi, Gracie. Beck minding the shop this morning?" Eric Morton smiled.

"Yep, though I'm sure it's slow," I answered. "The whole town's here."

Except for Reggie McFerrin. The saloon owner was nowhere to be seen. It could be that 10 a.m. was too early for him, a night owl, to be up and about. It seemed odd that the four-time former mayor would not show up to an important community meeting.

Then to my surprise, Elana walked through the door. She smiled at me and immediately made her way to the cinnamon roll trays. She grabbed a roll and a napkin.

"I didn't know you were coming to this," I said, as I filled a cup of coffee for her.

"I told my boss about what's going on in town." She smiled and took the coffee gratefully. "He thought it was important for me to be here and gave me the morning off."

"I'll be sitting with my dad, and it looks like he's on the right side near the front. You want to sit with us? I'll be in soon."

When the influx of people slowed, I downed the rest of the coffee in my cup and prepared to go inside. As I was consolidating the leftover cinnamon rolls into one tray, a shadow fell across the table. I took in my breath. A feeling of dread rumbled in my stomach. Anxious thoughts buzzed through my brain. The words of the attorney's letter flashed before my eyes.

You and your establishment.... The Laughing Loaf.... Negligence.

"Nate Behrens." I took in my breath, then looked up to see the man standing in front of me. He seemed to have had the same idea as my dad. Today he'd ditched the REI pants, boots and fleece pullover for a blue dress shirt and a button-down vest. His dark hair was combed back into a small ponytail, and he'd trimmed his beard. I didn't want to admit it, but he'd cleaned up nicely.

He glanced at me, then his eyes darted away. He also looked nervous. Though maybe part of it was that he was standing in front of the person he was in the process of suing.

"Can I – get some coffee?" He shifted on his feet. His normally tanned face looked unusually pale. "I'm getting up to talk today. About my brother. I don't like speaking in front of people, but the mayor thought it would be helpful."

I poured him a cup, though he could have easily gotten it himself. I handed it to him.

"I'm sure you'll be fine," I said dismissively and scanned the doors for incoming attendees. My face felt warm. I wished he'd go away.

"Thank you." He nodded, a pained look in his eyes, then went inside the theatre.

Minutes later, I heard the squawk of a mic being turned on, then Mayor C thanking everyone for coming. I entered the auditorium and moved down toward the front to take my seat next to my dad and Elana.

Both Mayor C and the chief had a podium on the stage of the old theatre, which had been built in the 1920s. Libraries smell of old wood and musty pages, an invitation to pull a book from the shelf and sit down and enter a new world; theatres smell of paint and wood and decades of sweat and make-up from the years of shows, concerts, meetings, and graduations in them.

You can smell the excitement, the anticipation from all the years of people on the stage under the lights and in the audience. Someone's shining moment. Someone's carefully practiced debut. Heated debates about very important subjects long since lost to time. Carefully crafted speeches that touched hearts and brought tears or rallying cries.

The polished wooden stage shone from the light coming in from the spotlights above. The theatre was nearly full—I estimated more than 150 people, men, women, and children. Some of them second and third generation River Grovians, some of them who settled here as adults. Most River Grove residents had taken time to be here today, whether that meant taking off work or shutting down their business for a couple of hours—a sign that the past week had made an impact on them.

Mayor C took a sip of water from a paper cup on the podium.

"Chief Westerman and I called this meeting to talk about the situation in River Grove. We've had a couple of serious crimes take place in the past week." She cleared her throat. "I know this is unfamiliar for you all. This is not something we've dealt with in our small community for many years. Today, Dave and I will share the progress on the cases so far. We also want to ask for your help and talk about the issue of crime prevention."

I was impressed. Corrinne Webster wasn't always the most touchy-feely person, but she was doing what she should be doing right now—showing leadership during a hard time.

"On Thursday night, at approximately 2 a.m. there was a break-in at Speed Spot Motor Works, as I'm sure you all know. Two catalytic converters were stolen, as well as a work laptop in a customer's car with some sensitive information on it. Chief Westerman is working on the case, and

I'd like to hand the mic over to him now, so he can update you."

There was a high-pitched metallic screech as Chief Westerman took the mic.

"To some of you," and the chief seemed to be looking at the seats in front of us, where Jake and Jeanne sat, "it may seem like the burglary at Speed Spot got lost in the shuffle after the murder of Mr. Behrens. But I'm happy to announce this morning that we have made some progress in the case."

As he said this, I saw Jake Daniels sit up abruptly in his seat and lean forward.

"I was able to notify BlueSurf Technologies in Santa Cruz this morning that the stolen laptop has been recovered."

There were some *whoops* and a few isolated claps from the audience, but not much more.

A man's voice called out, and it wasn't Jake.

"Have you made an arrest, Dave?" I looked to the opposite side of the theatre, in the direction of the voice, but couldn't figure out who it was.

The chief cleared his throat. "We have not at this time. We are pursuing leads, both in River Grove and throughout the county. We will keep you all notified of any developments."

"You don't have the manpower in town to solve this case." This was Jake, and now he was standing up. "Admit it, Dave. You guys can't handle this. I've been waiting to hear from you, and I've just spent almost three grand on a new security system—"

Jeanne Daniels was looking up at her husband from her seat, whispering fiercely to him. Jake sat down.

The chief leaned in toward the mic and lowered his

voice. "Jake, you and I can handle this offline. This is not the time."

He cleared his throat. "I'd like to continue with an update on Nicholas Behrens' murder. We do have a report back from the medical examiner. "

Every sound, every movement in the theatre stopped.

With a rustle, the chief flipped the page on the stapled document he was holding.

"Mr. Behrens had a poison in his system, a neurotoxin—called *tetrodotoxin*. The cause of death was asphyxiation, since the poison moved through his body, finally paralyzing his diaphragm. He would have had a hard time talking and would eventually have gone into a coma then died."

On the video from my camera, Nico had been gasping. When he'd called for help, it had seemed like his lips weren't working right. He'd had trouble forming words.

I quickly picked up my phone and googled *tetrodotoxin*.

"You can't stay off your phone, even at a moment like this?" My father leaned toward me and whispered disapprovingly. I shrugged it off as I looked at the search results.

Tetrodotoxin is an extremely potent poison (toxin) found mainly in the liver and gonads of some fish, such as puffer fish, globefish, and toadfish (order Tetraodontiformes) and in some amphibian, octopus, and shellfish species.

And here we were in River Grove, fifteen minutes away from the ocean. From Santa Cruz, where most of these things could be acquired, fresh off the boat.

"This was a deliberate poisoning." Chief Westerman said, his eyes on the crowd, as the news settled in uncomfortably with all of us. "As we suspected, we are looking for a murderer. Someone whom we believe targeted Nico Behrens."

Mayor C shot a look at the chief and stepped up to the

mic. She took the mic out of its stand and walked out from behind the podium, to the center of the stage.

"Nico Behrens moved here from Los Angeles a month ago. Two nights ago, his body was found on the back step of The Laughing Loaf."

Seriously. Did she *have* to say that part?

"I've invited Nico's next of kin, Nate Behrens, to join us today and tell us about his brother." She gestured to Nate, who was sitting in the front row, off to the side.

Nate stood up and moved to the steps leading to the stage. Once he got up on stage and headed to the mic, he seemed to move in slow motion, as if putting off the task of speaking as long as possible. He had a piece of paper, which he placed on the podium, then picked up again and held, then laid down again.

When Mayor C handed him the mic, he froze for a second, his light blue eyes showing that deer-in-the-headlights look. The crowd, who had been murmuring during Mayor C's introduction, fell quiet. This man was a newcomer, a stranger. I'd seen River Grove both embrace and shut out newcomers. How would they treat Nate?

I wondered why I even cared; this man had put me in a difficult situation by taking legal action against me and all I'd shown him was sympathy. I'd even got him talking to the chief, which seemed to have jumpstarted the case and given them both an opportunity to share information.

Right now, all eyes were on Nate Behrens. He stood stiff like an obelisk of stone, staring out from the stage, mesmerized, probably terrified, by the crowd of townspeople.

He started out with a cough, then swallowed and looked around anxiously. Then he began talking, slowly at first, then he seemed to become more comfortable.

"The mayor asked if I'd talk about my brother. We're new in town, and she thought it would help you get to know —" Nate's face twisted up. Mayor C brought over a glass of water and a box of tissues.

"A month ago, my brother Nico and I moved here from Los Angeles. We were looking to get away from big city life. I'm a nature photographer and did some work on some documentaries in LA. My brother, Nico, had been working in modeling for five years. If he looked a little familiar to you, it's because you've probably seen his face. He was a plumber in an ad for drain cleaner. He's been in catalogs for clothing, for jewelry and—for underwear."

A murmur rippled through the audience. I heard someone laugh.

"Nico was my younger brother, but for a long time, I acted like his parent. When our parents were killed in a plane crash on a business trip, I'd just turned eighteen and Nico was ten. With the help of an aunt, I ended up raising my brother. It was a tough job."

Not the backstory I'd expected. It explained the protectiveness Nate felt for his brother.

Nate coughed and took a gulp from his glass of water. He took a deep breath, which I and everyone else could hear with crystal clarity through the microphone.

"To be honest, for most of his life, my brother was in trouble. He skipped school. He was always in detention. He was suspended from school several times. After he was caught twice stealing shoes from a department store, a judge sentenced him to time in a youth facility. I tried everything I could to help him—first I lectured him, which didn't do any good. I went to counseling sessions with him—while I worked to support us. Then one day, a woman spotted him in a mall with some friends and asked if he'd like a job. Nico dropped out of school when he was sixteen and ended up working some modeling gigs. He was very good at it—and he loved the work. Nico started to change. I think because he realized there was something he was good at. He was signed to a modeling agency and began making good money. Soon he was supporting us. He bought a house for us in LA and told me that he was hoping he could finally give back to me all the time and money I'd spent on him."

"At the beginning of this year, Nico was signed to do a series of ads for a Paris jeweler. For the shoot, he wore a pair of very expensive diamond cufflinks. The shoot went on for a week. When Nico went home after that last day, the cufflinks were missing."

A quiet had settled over the crowd in the theatre. It's as if someone had pressed pause; no one, not Mayor C or the chief, or anyone in the audience seemed to move.

Nate took another gulp of water, which could be heard loudly over the sound system. He rubbed his face.

"The police, the FBI, spent weeks talking to Nico, the photographer and the photographer's assistant—and anyone who'd visited the shoot. Our home was searched, taken apart, looking for those cufflinks. Even though Nico's juvenile records were sealed—he was still the prime suspect. Nico went in for hours of questioning. Still, they had no proof, no evidence that Nico had done it. He was released."

Nate started to tear up, and I could hear the hoarseness in his voice as he continued talking.

"The police pressed no charges. They found no evidence that Nico had done it. But Nico was tried over and over again in the press. Newspaper stories, magazines. A special on the evening Hollywood gossip show. Everyone assumed he must have done it. Nico's agency let him go. Even when he was out at the grocery store or getting coffee, he'd get taunted. He was out of work and miserable. He started to look to things he'd done in the past, drinking, the partying lifestyle he'd had in school. That's when I suggested we move out of LA. I looked for some place quiet and isolated. I found River Grove. After visiting, I felt this was the right place to start again."

Dang it. I found myself tearing up as Nate talked. Not only was it clear that Nate loved his brother, I also related to what he was saying about finding a place to start again. When I looked at my dad, I saw that he was crying—maybe he was feeling the same way. I dug a pack of tissues out of my purse and handed it to him.

All along my row, I saw people dabbing at their eyes. A few seats before me, Jake Daniels and his wife were sniffing loudly. Even Chief Westerman on stage was dabbing at his eyes.

"Chief Westerman told me to ask you. If you can think of anything you saw or heard regarding my brother that day, please let him know. My brother didn't deserve to die this way. I want to find his killer."

With a nod, he stepped away from the podium. Mayor C moved over to give him a hug, her tiny frame dwarfed by Nate's size.

The audience seemed not to know how to respond to this, but eventually a few claps started, then the entire audi-ence began clapping. A murmur of conversation was building in the room.

Mayor C made her way to the podium and reached up to pull the microphone down to her level.

"Thank you for that, Nate." She nodded at him in the front row.

"I want to let you know a few things we've been working on. First of all, we invite you to the town council meeting on Monday night, where we'll discuss crime fighting strategies in River Grove. We need your ideas, so I want to see a good turnout." She gave attendees a stern look. "Also, people. I want to reiterate what Nate just said. We have an anonymous tip line now, for any information you may have regarding Nico Behrens and anything you may have seen or heard that day. The number's on our town website, and chief Westerman will be handing out flyers as you leave. I also want to thank The Laughing Loaf and Gracie Markley for her generous contribution of coffee and cinnamon rolls today."

With that, people began to stand. Conversations sprung up all over the room, like clusters of seedlings around redwood trees in spring. All of this was huge news—the kind that this small town hadn't seen in decades.

The murmurs in the room turned to a low roar. I watched as Nate tried to make his way down the steps from the stage, only to be accosted by a group of older ladies who apparently wanted to console him. Mayor C had been right in asking him to tell his and Nico's story. I wouldn't be surprised if Nate ended up being invited for many nights of dinners. His acceptance in River Grove society had begun.

Part of me bristled at this. I felt sorry for Nate, but I was miffed at how he'd treated me. He hadn't just threatened to sue me. He was *doing* it. I felt like me and my business were taking the brunt of his anger and frustration at the murder of his brother.

"Well, that wasn't a bad meeting, don't you think?" My father turned to me. "You'd think someone would have heard or noticed something about Nico and his murder this week—it's a small town."

"But if someone did, you'd think we all know about it by now. It's impossible to keep news from spreading here." I wondered if I should call in my tip about Reggie McFerrin burying something by the river. I'd feel better about leaving it anonymously, though I wondered how "anonymous" anything could be in this town. I also wasn't sure the Chief would follow up on a tip regarding the exalted Reggie McFerrin.

Right then my stomach growled so loudly that my dad laughed. While preparing food for everyone else, I hadn't had the opportunity to eat.

"You better hope there's some cinnamon rolls left, dear."

We made our way up the aisle to the lobby. Just my luck, the pans of cinnamon rolls had been picked clean, so much so, that I wondered if people had come by to wipe out globs of cinnamon brown sugar butter with their fingers. I saw what looked like a big fingerprint. To be fair, I can't say I'd never been tempted.

I stacked the trays, while my dad took the nearly empty Cambros off the table and prepared to fold up the tablecloth.

"Hey, there, John and Gracie." Chief Westerman called out. "You guys need some help with those?" The chief waved over a reluctant Robert Loudon, who looked like he was hurrying to get to his car.

"Thanks, Dave, Robert." I nodded, as the two men each took one.

I walked close to the chief as I led the way to my car.

When we were far enough away from Robert Loudon and my father, I leaned toward the chief.

"So, tetrodotoxins come from seafood."

"Gracie, I can google, too." The chief said, annoyed. "I saw on the video how he was acting at the end. It reminded me of a case we had in Sacramento. A man who'd died after eating the wrong part of a pufferfish at a sushi restaurant. The chef was careless when he cut the fish."

"Do you know what Nico was doing that day?" I asked. "Where he ate lunch?"

"According to his brother, Nico left River Grove at about 10 a.m. that day and came back at 2:45 p.m.," the chief grunted as he shifted his grip on the Cambro. "It looks like he was in Capitola for part of that time—at a café down by the beach. The way he looks, he's a—uh—pretty noticeable guy." The chief finished that last sentence awkwardly.

Of course, he was. Those who'd seen Nico, remembered him.

"The café doesn't happen to serve seafood—" I opened the back hatch of the Subaru.

"They don't," the chief muttered as he hoisted the Cambro into the back of the car.

"Would it be that café on the beach by Rio del Mar?" I had the crazy thought that I could head down there. If it hadn't been the café where he'd encountered the poison, I could ask around and try to follow Nico's trail.

"And why should I tell you if it was?" The chief muttered as he pulled out his phone to check a message. "It's no business of yours, Gracie. Stay out of this."

With his answer, my thought was that it probably was exactly that café—which I'd seen on an outing with Biga and my father to the beach at Seacliff State Park.

After arranging to see some World War II memorabilia of my father's, Robert Loudon hoisted the other Cambro into the car.

"Thanks to both of you. The town needed this meeting." I nodded at the two men.

The chief grimaced and kicked the ground. "Thanks for

the refreshments," he said, begrudgingly. "And for filling me in on what happened with Nico Behrens in LA, Gracie."

"So, your meeting with Nate Behrens was helpful then?" I asked, though I knew I was pushing it.

"It was," he said gruffly.

I smiled politely, pleased that I'd made a difference. And that the chief had been forced to admit it.

Chapter Eleven

After a slow day at The Laughing Loaf, I came home with Biga and did some cuddling with him on the couch as I reread a favorite Agatha Christie mystery.

This morning I'd put ingredients for a bean chorizo soup into the crock pot, and from the smoky, spicy smell in the late afternoon, it was almost done. Mid-afternoon, the day had turned cold and damp, and the hearty soup topped with croutons made of day-old bread would be the perfect dinner.

I was right at the end of my book—at a time when I really did *not* want to be interrupted—when my father came into the room wearing another button-down shirt and sports coat. No tie, though.

"How do you think this looks?" He turned to the side and looked out into the imaginary distance, like a pose you'd see in a men's clothing catalog. Nico Behrens he was not. I tried not to laugh. "For going out to dinner, I mean."

I sat up on the couch, startling Biga from his curled position. "What? Tonight?"

He shook his head. "Not tonight. After the meeting today, Mary Jo Hartman and I were talking. She said she was interested in checking out a new steak house down in Santa Cruz. I'd heard of it, so I said I'd like to check it out, too. We'll go some night next week."

I must have been staring at him. Apart from friendly dinners with a few female colleagues at the university, my father hadn't really gone out since my mother had died. He hadn't seemed interested in dating anyone. But then maybe this wasn't a date. I tried to remember this woman. Had I met her?

"Who's Mary Jo?"

"She runs Growing Affection—you know that little plant nursery out at the edge of town. Her husband passed away last year. We talk when we see each other around town."

I remembered all the warnings, the grilling my father and I had gone through in WITSEC. We had to be careful about any involvements. No matter how close we came to someone, we couldn't reveal our identities. We couldn't talk about our past unless it was the rewritten backstory WITSEC had given us.

Could my absent-minded father be trusted to keep our secret? The possibilities scared me.

"You'll be careful, won't you?" I watched as he tried buttoning, then unbuttoning his sports jacket to see which looked better.

"Of course. We'll make sure to use protection." My father was trying to give me a hard time. He smiled mischievously. "We're going out because we both like steak. And each other's company."

Panic stirred in the pit of my stomach. "But you

remember what the marshals said. We have to be careful about getting too close—sharing too much—"

"I'm well aware of the need for caution, dear. I can handle it."

My father decided not to button. Then, emboldened by his choice, he undid the top button of his shirt. "As you used to tell me when you were four: *You're not the boss of me.*"

I did remember. Our roles seemed reversed now. I was the parent and my father the child. I worried about him, felt responsible for him. By marrying Ben, I'd dragged him into the tech spy aftermath, taking him away from his friends and his position at the university.

"I worry about you, father. That's all. I feel responsible—"

"You take on too much responsibility, Gracie." He smiled affectionately. "Ever since your mother passed away, you've felt you have to do everything you think she did. You think you messed up my life by marrying Ben." He turned to look at himself in the foyer mirror. "I feel relieved that I can say it now. I never liked the man. There was something about him that was...off."

"You didn't like him?" I sat upright and thought about this. My father and my ex-husband had never seemed to click. Wisely, he'd never said anything negative about Ben. He probably knew that would drive me even closer to the man. When the truth came out about my husband, he didn't once judge me for my choices.

"Don't feel guilty, dear." My father took his sports coat off and hung it on a hanger. "Believe me. I'm fine here. I don't need your protection as much as you think I do."

I walked into the kitchen to check on the soup in the crockpot. Biga and my father followed me, both of them drawn by the savory smells of dinner.

As I diced the dried sourdough into cubes for the croutons, I felt the stress of the past week weighing on me. I felt responsible for my father, responsible for my bakery. I was afraid our new life was going to fall through. That it was like a deck with a rotted board in it somewhere. We'd fall through as soon we stepped in the wrong place. It was just a matter of time.

I threw pats of butter into a frying pain and melted it, then tossed in the bread cubes. I seasoned them with garlic powder, oregano, and thyme.

"I received a letter yesterday," I suddenly blurted out. "From Nate Behrens' attorney. He's suing me and the bakery for negligence in his brother's death."

My dad paced the kitchen as he thought about this.

"That doesn't make any sense, Gracie. The case doesn't have a leg to stand on." He took his sport jacket off and hung it up on a hanger. "It wasn't him falling on your back step that killed him. I read up on tetrodotoxin after the meeting today. It's a neurotoxin. It blocks off the transmission of signals from the nervous system to the muscles. It gradually paralyzes the lungs, and the victim goes into respiratory arrest. Nothing could have helped Nico Behrens at that point, even if you had heard him back there. He was in the last stages of poisoning."

When my father explained it that way—it sounded true. Reasonable.

I needed to get this worry off my plate. This suit was all about Nate's grief at his brother's death. Nate felt he'd failed his parents for not protecting Nico, just as I'd thought I failed my father by marrying Ben.

He was looking for some way to offload that failure onto someone or something else. Which I could relate to. It was a heavy load.

I stirred the croutons in the pan as they began to brown in the butter. Biga was staring up at me hopefully, as if to say: *You drop one, I'm on it.*

"You're right. This is not my fault." I looked up at my father. I felt things lightening already.

I was tired of living in fear.

After dinner, I would drive down to Nate Behrens' house and have a talk with him.

The smoky, spicy flavor of the soup turned out to be just what we needed on this cold and dreary night. After my dad and I'd finished dinner, I loaded the dishwasher and tidied the kitchen.

Then I washed up, brushed my hair, and looked at myself in the mirror a little too long. *Why do you think Nate Behrens will care—or even notice—how your hair looks? The guy sees you in the same light as his brother's killer.*

The Behrens place was a white one story not far from the riverbank.

A small dock on the property jutted into the river, which was slower moving here than it was downtown. Another, smaller building stood next to the house, over-looking the river.

As I got closer, I saw bags of cement and stacks of wood up against the small building. Beck had said the Behrens were turning the small building into a studio for Nate's photography.

The front door had been painted a bright brick red. I knocked. After waiting a few minutes without a response, I considered the idea of leaving and not talking to Nate at all.

Soon I saw a single, light-blue eye look through the middle of the three small windows set in the door.

After a pause, the door opened, and there stood Nate Behrens, in jeans and a brown sweatshirt.

"Yes?" His face was expressionless, except for those eyes which bored into me.

"I want to speak with you, Nate." I stood firmly on the porch. He looked like he really wanted me to go away, or he seriously hoped today's stiff wind would blow me off his porch and back into town.

"If this is about the legal action, you'll have to speak to my attorney. Peter James Jordan." He said matter-of-factly. "All inquiries should go to him."

If he'd shut the door in my face right then, I wouldn't have been surprised.

"Wait a minute. There's something I need to say to you, Nate." I glared right back at him. "Your claim that I was negligent in your brother's death is not true. Nico fell on those steps because he'd been poisoned. I am sorry, but even if I'd heard him, I could not have helped him."

Nate just stood staring at me.

"Also, I watched the video from my camera from that evening and from what I saw he was barely whispering."

When Nate blinked and took in his breath suddenly; I was talking about the last moments of his brother's life.

"Would you like to come in, Ms. Markley?"

He opened the door wider, and I followed him into the room.

What I saw beyond him was a tidy living room, with a view of the river through a large bay window. Sleek wood furniture, unadorned with any clutter, gave the room a modern feel. Rows of framed photos filled the walls.

I'd hoped this would be a quick conversation on the doorstep. I did not want to talk long to this guy. My intention had been to tell him to back off and drop the suit and then leave.

"I was just making some coffee." He said matter-of-factly, as if I was a roommate or friend who'd dropped by. "Care for some?"

I swallowed. "Okay."

I looked up at the rows of photography—most of them birds, some caught midflight, some in their nests, in trees, and floating on lakes. I wanted to get up and examine them more closely.

Focus, Gracie. You came here for a reason.

I heard hissing noises and a spurt coming from the kitchen—the familiar sounds of a high-quality espresso machine, the kind that had set me back $2000 when I'd purchased it for Laughing Loaf.

I caved and walked around the living room, checking out the photos. I spent a long time looking at a very thin, bright white bird with a crooked neck, perched on a branch hanging out over the river. A shadow fell on its feathers, revealing intricate detail and texture. The bird was so striking, such a contrast to its surroundings, I couldn't stop looking at it.

A few minutes later, Nate brought back a cappuccino with thick foam on top.

I took a sip of the coffee, and it reminded me of something. A trip with Ben and an amazing breakfast on the Serengeti. The coffee was rich and earthy, a blend from Kenya. I remembered a safari where we came face to face with elephants. Giraffes. Nostalgia filled me. Then anger, as I remembered how Ben had financed this trip.

I took a deep breath and returned to the present. To the

house of the man who was in the process of trying to ruin my business.

"Nate, I understand how you must feel about your brother. Especially after you basically raised him. But there is no way I could have helped him that night, even if I did hear him on the back step. Please stop this." As I pleaded, I thought of something. "Nate, did the chief show you the video from the back camera at Laughing Loaf?"

He shook his head then swallowed. "He said I shouldn't see it."

"Do you want to see it?" I watched as different emotions moved across his face. I did feel he had a right to see it, but it might be more than he could handle. "It's on my computer at the bakery."

He frowned and stared out the window at the reflection of lights on the river.

"I'd like to see it," he said firmly, his face tightening. He flexed his hands then went to the hallway to grab his backpack.

I drove him to The Laughing Loaf in my car. For the most part, he sat quietly as we drove. He smelled of freshly cut pine wood and the coffee he'd been brewing. Both scents reminded me of Seattle, and I felt a wave of home-sickness.

As I followed the highway into downtown, something stopped ahead in the middle of the empty road and glared at us, its eyes glowing eerily silver in the darkness. I jumped, sucked in my breath, and got ready to brake. Then it scut-tled across the road

"Holy crap!" I breathed, my heart pounding as I clutched the wheel. "What was that?"

Next to me, Nate chuckled softly.

"It's a coyote. A young one. He was scared of us." In my

peripheral vision, I saw him looking over at me with curiosity. "You aren't from around here, are you?"

I swallowed and kept to the story line I'd memorized and been grilled on for months.

"We moved here from Portland. My dad and I lived in an old house off Hawthorne Avenue." It rolled off my tongue so easily now. "It was in the city, so we didn't see many—uh, *critters*. Except for raccoons rifling through our garbage cans."

"Nico and I grew up in a canyon near LA." Nate said in a calm, conversational tone I hadn't heard from him yet. He'd either been angry at me or nervous at the prospect of public speaking at the theatre. "Miles of forests, animals everywhere. It wasn't till our parents died that we moved to the suburbs, to live with my aunt in the San Fernando Valley. Nico was younger, so the transition was easier for him. I missed exploring the woods."

"You must like being in River Grove." He had lots of room to explore here. And lots of wildlife to photograph.

A haze seemed to fall over Nate. He stared out the window and became quiet again.

When we pulled up next to the front entrance of The Laughing Loaf, the place was dark except for the distant glow of the lights I kept on overnight in the front counter and baking area. I unlocked the door, and we went back to my closet of an office. The room was meant for one person; I suddenly felt awkward. I wished I had a laptop I could take out and we could watch in the wide-open safety of the dining area.

Nate shifted on his feet and looked around nervously as I moved my computer mouse over the folder for the recordings. I saw the file and highlighted it.

"Please, come have a seat in here," I stepped back,

outside of the small cubby of a room. He should be sitting down to watch this. I'd opened up a folder with the video file in it.

"Click on that file."

From outside the cubby, I could hear the recording—Nico's footsteps approaching down the alley—and I saw Nate's head and back as he began to watch. He gripped the arms of the chair and seemed to take in a breath.

As the recording continued, Nate's back grew more rigid. Then slowly, toward the end of the clip, as Nico fell and lay on the back step of the bakery, Nate seemed to sink lower in the seat. At the end, he slumped down, his head in his hands.

Instantly, I felt sorry I'd suggested this. He'd said he wanted to see it, but the chief hadn't shown him—maybe for good reason.

I wondered if my motivation had been selfish, only to show Nate that I had nothing to do with his brother's death. That I could not have possibly heard Nico's muffled cries outside the bakery. That I was the nice person willing to help him, so he'd drop his suit.

Nate sat that way for a few minutes, slumped into the seat. Then he stood up and pushed the chair back. He didn't even look at me.

"Thank you, Gracie," he said under his breath. I stared at him. He'd always called me Ms. Markley.

"Let me drive you back." I scrambled to grab my purse and keys.

"*No.*" His voice came out with some force, deep and guttural. "I'll walk."

He hoisted his backpack over his shoulder and walked slowly out the back door of my bakery into the dark alley.

Chapter Twelve

With my regrets about showing Nate the video, I didn't sleep great that night.

The next morning, I dragged myself out of bed in the dark. Biga scowled and hunkered down in the warm bed, refusing to join me.

The prospect of hunting down Reggie McFerrin's buried "treasure," along with a triple-shot latte, did a good job of propelling me through the day.

After I closed up at 2 p.m., Elana met me at the back entrance of Laughing Loaf.

She was dressed casually in jeans and a t-shirt since she was off work for President's Day—something I did not get in food service.

This would be an adventure.

"I brought a trowel," Elana said, pulling a short-handled tool from her backpack. "Kirk used it for digging toilets when he went camping with his family. Don't worry, that's before the toilets were used."

I looked over at her and grinned. "Glad you clarified that."

We followed the alley until we got to the dirt and pine-needle-strewn cutoff for the path along the river. Unfortunately, there were a lot of other people who thought a walk along the river would be a good idea today. A dad and his young son stood on the bank while the son tried to skip rocks across the water. We waved and smiled to a few people I remembered seeing in the bakery.

"Any plan for your legal troubles?" Elana asked as we started to get into a rhythm. Elana had longer legs than I did, and she was not my dog—we were going much faster down the path than Biga and I did yesterday. I looked to my left at the backs of the downtown businesses. Most were closed today, including Speed Spot. The Riverside wasn't due to open till 4 p.m. Hopefully, we had a window of time in which to do our digging unobserved.

I grimaced and shot her a look. I told her I'd invited Nate to watch the video clip of his brother's death—and that I regretted it now.

Elana stopped and pulled her water bottle out to take a drink. "You didn't force him. He wanted to see it, and the chief refused to show him. Maybe he'll see he was wrong about you being negligent."

"It upset him," I said, remembering him sinking lower into my office chair as he watched it. "He left without a word and walked home."

"Doesn't mean it was a bad thing for him to see it," Elana said matter-of-factly.

At this point, the land to our left rose higher in elevation, as the path following the river started to turn away from downtown. I looked up to see the outdoor deck of The Riverside, shaded with a tarp, and the stairs Reggie McFerrin had come down with his shovel.

I looked around and recognized the stump, the fallen

branch, and the soft, mulchy ground I'd seen yesterday. Pine needles had fallen on it and leaves from a nearby oak on The Riverside's property. But I knew: this was the place.

"Let's dig."

Elana started scooping at the dirt with the trowel. After a few minutes, she stood up, flexing her hands in pain. I took the trowel and continued, till we had gone almost a foot in. We didn't see anything, until the dirt softened and crumbled at the side of the hole, and I saw we we'd been a few inches off the mark. In the dirt, there was the corner of something that looked like white paper. I dug deeper until Elana reached in and pulled out an envelope.

"Nothing written on it." She pulled off her backpack and searched in a side compartment. She took out a pocketknife to neatly slit the envelope open.

"Somebody's prepared," I laughed.

Inside was a folded note. She opened it, and we both looked at it.

It was an eviction notice for unit 19 of the River Grove Trailer Park.

Dated the day before Nico's death.

Chapter Thirteen

The next morning, I moved around the back room, doing what I usually did to prep and bake, but I moved at the speed of a banana slug.

Even though I had come in early, at 5 a.m., I felt about an hour behind, dividing up tubs of bulk dough into bannetons for their final rise, and pulling scones out of the freezer to bake.

I was overthinking things this morning. Off my game.

I hadn't slept much the night before. The past few days had been intense: the town meeting, and Elana's and my treasure hunt. Then my invitation to Nate to watch the camera footage. I kept remembering Nate's head, as he watched the video of his brother stumbling down the alley.

Maybe it was in sympathy with me, but Biga didn't seem to sleep well either. As soon as I brought him in, he walked slowly across the floor to his bed, curled up and slept through most of the morning.

I laid out the rectangles of cinnamon roll dough and had them ready, so that when Beck came in, she could top them with filling, roll them up and cut them. We'd be ready to roll —pun intended.

After waking up from two hours asleep on the sofa, drool on the pillow and Biga wedged in next to my feet, I knew exactly what today's joke would be.

I typed it up and sent it to the printer. Then cut it for posting on the Joke of the Day stand on the counter.

The Laughing Loaf Joke of the Day
Have you heard about corduroy pillows?
They're making headlines.

At 7 a.m., Beck came in singing softly to herself, swinging a basket by her side. I never knew what mood Beck would be in. Generally, she was a happy, optimistic young woman, but Nico's murder had affected her deeply.

Today she seemed in good spirits.

"I tried baking something last night." There was excitement in her eyes as she took the cloth napkin off the basket. "I was feeling a little down about what's going on in town, so I looked through old cookbooks to find something to make. Sometimes it cheers me up, you know?"

"I *do* know." I smiled as I thought of my dad and I baking during my teen years. "That's what I've been doing for twenty years. It always makes me feel better."

Beck got a plate and with tongs put on it two golden fried squares dusted with powdered sugar.

I suspected what they were right away. She passed me the plate.

"Beignets. Beck, these look great." I took a bite out of one and moaned. Fried sugary goodness. These were really good. "Beck, what made you think of making beignets?"

"I was watching a show about Mardi Gras in New

Orleans. I got inspired." Becky pulled one out of the basket and bit into it. "Sam ate, like maybe *five* last night. I didn't want to leave them at home."

Beignets would be a great addition to our morning repertoire. I liked the idea of Beck coming up with a signature item on the menu. The kitchen was set up for baking, not fried foods, but we did have a gas stove and a pot for frying.

"Let's include this as a limited time item on the menu, to start with anyway. You bring in your recipe, and let's see what we need to order. I remember that you mix the dough up the night before, raise it in the fridge, then fry them the next morning. You'd need to come in when I come in."

Beck brown eyes lit up. "Really? This can be on the menu?"

I nodded. "How about decorating the place for Mardi Gras for their debut?"

The wheels were already turning in Beck's head. "Streamers, maybe some of those colorful beads. I'll check the party store in Santa Cruz."

It's pretty easy to bring employee satisfaction. After working for tech companies for years, it boggled my mind. Why don't managers figure this out? It's not as much about perks like free lunches or car washes and dentist appointments on site. Pay them decently, of course. Give them a chance to be part of the process, part of the product. Let them contribute to a company's success. Let their ideas shine.

As customers came in and I served coffee and pastries, my mind drifted to Nate last night. I don't think I'd been wrong in offering to show him the video. At the same time, he'd seen his brother's last moments and had been devastated by it.

If I was serious about finding Nico's killer, it was time to act. I remembered what I'd heard from the chief about Nico's day leading up to his death. I was still exhausted from my lack of sleep, but I wanted to follow his route that day and learn about his time on the coast before he ended up at The Riverside.

I went back to my computer closet, googled the model's name, and printed out a nice, clear picture of him. People would remember that face.

By 9 a.m., The Laughing Loaf was filling up with both regulars and new faces I remembered from the meeting in the theatre. People were coming in to mingle. The dining area was packed, and the tables outside in the front were nearly full, with people talking over coffee, their dogs lapping at the water-filled dog dishes I'd set out.

I scanned the crowd for Nate, but there was no sign of him.

Mayor C and the chief were at a corner table in the dining room, leaning in toward each other conspiratorially. I'd give anything to listen in, but I had no good excuse.

I went back behind the counter, where Beck was in the zone, filling coffee orders with a machine-like efficiency—a very cheerful efficiency.

I knew she'd left her bag of beignets in the back room. I came up behind her and asked if I could take two. She looked across the room and saw the mayor and the chief and nodded at me.

"I'll get them," she said quietly, while setting down two drinks for waiting customers at the end of the counter. "Wait—let me prepare a tray for them. Give me a few minutes. I'll make it special."

Meanwhile, I stopped at the coffee supplies stand across from the two officials to tidy up after the morning rush. I took my time rearranging the nutmeg, cocoa, sugar, and straw containers, pretending to be completely absorbed in the task. I opened the cabinet doors below to replace the half-filled trash bag.

"—said Nico Behrens had been asking for a jeweler who did custom work... willing to pay a high price for the job."

Holy crap. What if Nico *had* taken the jewels? What if he'd been trying to have the cufflinks broken down, maybe disassembled to fence more easily?

If he had contacted a jeweler about the cufflinks, he was taking a big risk. If news got out, any number of people could be after Nico. And not just the police.

As I shuffled straws from one container to the next, the two looked around them and I could feel their eyes on me. Voices went down to a whisper.

"—somewhere down in Santa Cruz... tracking the guy down... taking a trip to Europe this week—business in Belgium."

Belgium. *Brussels.* Maybe, Nico had met with a jeweler in town, asking for help in repurposing the diamond cuff links. After that, the jeweler would have poisoned Nico and taken off for the biggest diamond markets in the world.

Beck's voice infiltrated my thoughts.

"Gracie!" She called softly from the counter. When I walked over, she had beignets laid out neatly on a plate, re-dusted with fresh powdered sugar and a sprig of mint, on a tray with two smaller versions of the drinks the mayor and the chief had ordered—an oat milk latte and a raspberry white chocolate macchiato, the most sugary drink we make.

"You're amazing, Beck." Then I lowered my voice. "I'm trying to hear what I can from the two about the case."

Beck's eyes widened as she wrote a name on a customer's cup. "I hope you get some information."

I took the tray over to the two in the corner, trying to look friendly and solicitous.

"The two of you have been working so hard this week. This is for you, compliments of the Laughing Loaf."

The chief brightened, smiling and patting his belly. "Thank you, Gracie. Are these beignets? This is quite a treat."

Mayor C, however, was not placated by the food and beverage offerings. She looked me over suspiciously, like she was sure I'd slipped something into her latte. "Yes, so *nice* of you, Gracie."

When the two of them were leaving an hour later, Mayor C came up to me as I wiped down a table.

"Listen, Gracie. If you overheard *any* of that conversation, make sure you keep it to yourself." She hissed. "This case is not something for you to meddle in."

What I wanted to say was, *Then maybe you shouldn't talk about a murder investigation in a public place.*

I kept my mouth shut and smiled.

She gave me a warning look in return, then dropped her cup and plate in the bussing bin and walked out looking like a tiny yellow Lego figure come to life.

* * *

At 12:30, now that the customers dwindled to three, Beck and I sat at a table in the dining area and ate egg salad sandwiches I'd made on leftover brioche.

Beck brought me a new latte with a loaf-like image floating in the foam on top. The loaf shape was pretty clear —she'd gotten that part down. But the loaf looked—very unhappy. His face was reminiscent of Edvard Munch's painting *Scream*.

"You nailed the loaf." I smiled as I took a sip. "But he looks like he's having a very bad day."

Beck gave me a good-natured smile and adjusted her fountain of hair ponytail. "Yeah, I know. It does look like he's screaming. But I'm working on it."

I thought about whether I should talk to Beck about my little investigation.

"I'm going to over to Santa Cruz to check some things out today, after I close up," I said, as I lifted the sandwich to my mouth.

Beck got that smile she gets when she's very excited about something, but knows she needs to keep it on the down low. It's the look a cartoon cat gets after swallowing a mouse. Which convinced me I could tell her at least some of what I intended to do. She'd heard the news of Nico's trip along the coast on the day he died.

"You're going to find out what Nico did that day," she said almost whispering.

I raised my eyebrows as I continued chewing my sandwich.

"I'm going to follow up on what I heard from the mayor and the chief." I took a sip of my latte. The taste was perfect; Beck was a pro with the espresso machine. "I'm going to ask around. Figure out where he went and who he talked to that day."

I glanced at the clock on the wall of the dining area. It was 12:40 now. It would take me about 20 minutes to get to Santa Cruz to start questioning jewelers.

"Gracie, why don't you leave now? I can close down today." Beck's eyes shone with a new confidence. "It's slow and I can handle everything—and you can get on the highway before commuters start coming back over the hill. You'll have more time."

Beck could take care of the later customers before closing, and she could clean up. She could even mix cinnamon roll dough. I would need to come back later to get bread dough mixed and loaves in the proofer, but there was nothing I needed to do between now and then that Beck couldn't do.

"Thank you." I said, grateful for her suggestion. Maybe this was more opportunity for Beck to step up to the plate. She was capable of it. As long as she didn't start selling screaming lattes in my absence, Laughing Loaf was in good hands.

I called my father to let him know I'd be bringing Biga home, and he was fine with that. He didn't ask any questions as to where I was going, and I didn't volunteer any information. The less my dad knew about what I was doing, the better, especially if he was going to be talking to his new lady friend soon.

As I sat in the car after dropping off Biga, I texted Elana. I did it for two reasons—I wanted someone to know where I'd be, in the event I didn't come back. And I wanted to be able to touch base with her during the trip, to bounce my thoughts off someone.

> Heading to Santa Cruz to ask questions
> about Nico's last day

> You go, girl! Ping me if you want to meet
> up for dinner. Kirk's up in San Francisco for
> work.

I drove out of the woods on twisting Highway 9, huge coastal redwoods looming over me on either side as I made my way to the coast. Once I pulled onto Highway 1, the grey-blue Pacific Ocean came into view. A line of surfers in wetsuits bobbed on their boards, tiny specks, out in the choppy waters.

Away from the shelter of the trees, the force of the wind made my Subaru shudder. It was funny how different the weather could be as soon as you hit the coast. Often, everything changed once the ocean came into view.

I'd printed out a list of jewelers in Santa Cruz and ordered it by most likely places Nico would visit to ask about having the diamonds reset. Chain store jewelers were out; Nico would probably have looked for smaller, independent shops that did custom work.

In a box in a small satin bag in my purse, I had the engagement ring Ben had given me the year after our graduation—in case I needed it for a cover story. It was beautiful —a one-carat oval diamond in a silver setting, on a thin band set with tiny diamonds that almost looked like stars orbiting the oval.

I kept it because I felt I'd earned it. And it seemed more legitimate. As far as I knew, Ben had actually saved money to buy this; he'd purchased this before he'd gotten connected with his secrets-for-pay scheme. I hadn't worn it since I'd left Seattle. Today, it would get me some attention, and hopefully some information, from the shops I visited.

Vintage Sparkle was first on my list, a small shop downtown, off Pacific Avenue. I parked on a side street and walked to the tiny shop, next to a Persian rug store. The front window was lined with stickers boasting about its security systems.

A bell signaled my entry. I looked over cases of rings and necklaces in some unusual designs. Some had an art deco look, as if they could have been worn by flappers or movie stars in the 1920s. A few rings featured gemstones so big they seemed completely impractical. I certainly couldn't wear any of them while working in the bakery, and I couldn't imagine anyone doing any type of work involving their hands while wearing them.

The bell had summoned a tiny, middle-aged man wearing a black suit and a white tie over a striped black and white shirt. He looked like a singer in a barbershop quartet.

"Good afternoon, miss—"

"Call me Gracie," I smiled at the man. "I hear you do gemstone resettings."

"We do. And I'm Mark. Mark Justus." A black and white cat came out from behind the showcase and rubbed up against my legs. "What type of gem do you have?"

I hesitated. I didn't want to bring out the ring unless this was going somewhere. "It's a diamond. One carat. From my engagement ring. It's a lovely stone. The marriage didn't go so well, so I'd like to retool the stone in a completely new piece of jewelry. To make the best out of something with bad memories. My friend said you might be able to help."

The man smiled sympathetically. "And was your friend a customer here?"

"He said he'd stopped by here. Here's his picture."

"Oh, *my*." The old man shuddered as he looked at the photo. "Yes, he was here not long ago. A week ago, maybe. I felt a little uncomfortable when he told me about his piece of jewelry. I referred him to some other jewelers in town."

"Really?" I feigned surprise. "Was it something that your shop couldn't handle? Nicholas didn't mention this to me. I would have looked somewhere else—"

Mark Justus looked concerned. His store probably didn't get much traffic and he didn't want to turn away business. "No, no. I had concerns about the provenance of the stones. I—uh, try use an abundance of caution when people bring in large stones." The man gave me an odd look, as the cat left me and rounded the end of the display cabinet.

"I'm sorry to hear that. I can show you what I have." Hoping to distract him, I took the box out of the satin pouch and opened it on the glass counter. Mr. Justus held the box up and looked at it closely.

"Lovely clarity and color." He said, impressed. "A little bow tie effect—but not much. That's when you can see the light refracted inside the diamond; the effect looks a bit like a bow tie. This would make a lovely pendant, and we could certainly do the work."

I stood for a minute or two, looking over some of the pieces in the case, pretending to make up my mind. "I think I'll look around a little more. But I may be back."

The old man looked a little sad as I put the box back in the pouch and into my purse.

I headed for my car and sat down to map out the other stores on my list.

The woman at the counter in Heartstones, a new-agey jewelry store on Mission Street, hadn't seen anyone looking like Nico. The shop had an old hippie vibe, with lots of turquoise Southwestern-influenced jewelry and crystals. It didn't look like a place Nico would even go into.

DeValle Jewelers over near UC Santa Cruz hadn't seen anyone like Nico come in.

It was now nearing 2 p.m. Having gotten up at 4:30, I was in desperate need of coffee. I'd check the next place on my list and if that didn't pan out, I'd get coffee then head for the café in Aptos where Nico had been seen.

Raymond Steele Jewelers was a small shop next to a strip

mall not far from Pleasure Point, a popular surfing area. It was a bright, tidy shop in an old white clapboard house that looked recently renovated. A woman around my age stood behind the counter thumbing through some kind of a reference book.

She greeted me with a smile and instantly put down her book.

"How may I help you?"

I don't know what it was. Maybe that this person was my age, my demographic. I decided to change my tactics. I didn't need to trot out the engagement ring.

"I'm tracing the path of a friend of mine, who was in town looking for a jeweler last week." I smiled and introduced myself. "Tall, good-looking guy."

The young woman looked at me blankly and shook her head. Her lips tightened.

"Ms. Markley, I'm afraid we don't give out information about clients or prospective clients. Especially not to someone just walking in off the street."

I pulled the photo out of my purse and put it down on the counter. When she looked at it, her eyes widened. She hesitated for a moment, then let out her breath.

"Okay, *that* guy. He was here. Last Thursday. Late morning. You don't forget a face like that."

"Can you tell me what he was looking for?"

"He was looking for a reset. A pair of large diamonds. He was willing to pay well." She raised an eyebrow. "He kept emphasizing that."

"Did he show you the diamonds?"

She shook her head. "I don't think he had the stones with him. There was something about him that was—off. The size of the stones seemed way too good to be true. He told me the diamonds' size—ten carats a piece, which was outrageous. I thought he was exaggerating. But then, the guy also looked like he was a runway fashion model, so—"

"He was." I nodded grimly.

The woman did a double take. "Do you mean he's dead?"

"He was murdered last Thursday. His body was found on the back step of my bakery in River Grove."

"Mom! Come out here." The woman called toward a back room.

An older woman came through a curtained partition and joined us. She looked down at the photo.

"Oh, yeah. The guy gave his name as Skyler something. He was a real looker." She gave her daughter a glance of concern.

"This is my mother, Rosamond Steele," the younger woman smiled. "I'm Rachel—the Ray. Together we're Raymond Steele."

A mother-daughter jewelry business. I'm sure the Raymond Steele name gave the store a timeless, traditional appeal. A name you could trust. At the time it made me sad that two qualified women had to present their business under a man's name to succeed.

"Skyler was Nico. Nicholas Behrens. He was suspected in the theft of some very expensive diamond cufflinks at a photo shoot in LA, but he was never charged." I told them the story of the disappearance of the cufflinks during Nico's photo shoot.

"We could do a little research," Ray looked at her mother, who nodded. "To see if any stones of that size have appeared on the market recently. If he was smart, he'd be careful about revealing anything about the size or quality of the stones. He'd definitely get attention."

"If he did take the stones, it's amazing that he was questioned, and his house searched but he was never caught. He had to have been smart," I looked down at the photo of Nico, a man with a too-good-to-be-true face, trying to hide a pair of too-good-to-be-true diamonds. Did he have help? My thoughts went to Nate. Had he known the truth about Nico and the diamonds?

What if he'd helped hide them?

I thought about the conversation I'd overhead between the chief and the mayor.

"Can you think of any jeweler who would have been open to helping Nico with the diamonds—and maybe would have been tempted to take them himself?"

Ray and Rosamond's eyes connected, and Rosamond smiled.

"Of course. Jeff Cantwell," Rosamond said, nodding. "Jeff's had a shop down by the boardwalk for years. He's—well, let's just say he's an opportunist. He makes a decent amount of money at it. I wouldn't be surprised if he was all too willing to help Nico."

Ray looked up the business on her phone.

"Give me your number and I'll let you know if I find out anything."

I gave her my Laughing Loaf business card which had my cell number on it. She entered it into her contacts then sent me the link to Cantwell's business.

I thanked the women and set my GPS for Cliffside Jewelers.

Chapter Fourteen

The white tracks of the Santa Cruz Boardwalk's Giant Dipper coaster arched into the sky against the backdrop of dull grey clouds and a deserted sandy beach.

The brightly colored trams on the Skyride cables hung still, with the creepy fiberglass cavemen figures sitting in them. They'd be suspended there for a while. It was February, and the Santa Cruz Boardwalk wouldn't open till spring break.

When my phone GPS abruptly told me *YOU HAVE ARRIVED*, I realize I'd driven right past Cliffside Jewelers, which looked more like a pawn shop than a jewelry store. I turned the corner and found a parking spot on a side street.

The store window displayed bulky rings, chains and brooches that maybe suited a certain people's idea of adornment, but it certainly wasn't mine. The pieces lay on a swath of faded burgundy velour that had probably been sitting in the window for years.

An older woman with her white hair tied in a ponytail

came out to the counter. She looked like she wasn't a time waster, so I decided to be direct.

"I'm here for Jeff Cantwell. Is he in the store today?"

"He's not available right now." The woman said bluntly, as she tapped long, orange fingernails on the glass counter. "Who are you?"

"My name's Gracie. A friend of mine was here last week, and he recommended I ask Jeff about a diamond I wanted to have reset. You do that here, right?"

"Sometimes." The woman's voice drifted off, as if she were already bored with talking to me. "These days we're more into buying gems."

"Here's my friend. He looks a little like a model." I flashed Nico's photo. The woman's eyes opened so wide, they looked like they might pop out. I smiled at her. "I might be up for selling my one carat. But I'd have to think about it."

"We buy, no questions asked." The woman recited it in a sing song tone, as if she said it often. "We hold your stones until they're verified. We pay cash. Keeps it simple for everybody."

"I bet you see some large, beautiful stones come through here." I continued. She wasn't going for it.

There was more than a hint of suspicion in the woman's eyes, so I decided it was time to leave.

But I knew Nico had been there.

What I didn't know was whether he'd sold Jeff Cantwell the cufflinks.

* * *

I went back to my car and texted Elana.

Just met with a sketchy jeweler - Nico's definitely been here.

Headed to Cafe in Aptos, then coming back. How about dinner in River Grove?

Clouds were knotting into low, dark clumps along the coast. The air felt cold and damp, as if it were going to rain soon. I shivered as I started my car.

Fat drops of rain splatted on my windshield. I plugged in the café's address, and got onto Highway 1, heading for the beachside community of Aptos.

Traffic was building up on Highway 1, and on top of that, the right lane was blocked for road work.

While I forged ahead in stop-and-go traffic, not too patiently, I went over what I knew so far.

Nico had gone to at least three jewelry stores in Santa Cruz, asking about resetting or possibly selling some very large diamonds. The last store he went to was Jeff Cantwell's. Had Nico sold the cufflink diamonds—and if so, where was the cash? From the responses I'd gotten, he didn't seem to have had cufflinks with him.

I hoped Ray and Rosamond would carry through on their promise to check for news of any sale that could be the cufflinks. If Jeff Cantwell had gone to Brussels to sell the diamonds, maybe he had reset them or had them recut.

Rain poured down now, slowing traffic even more. I wondered if it was worth it to continue on to Rio del Mar. What information was I expecting to get there?

I glanced down at my GPS. At this point, it would take me a while to get off Highway 1 and head back in the other direction. I might as well stay put.

Thirty minutes later, I pulled off onto Spreckels Drive and headed down the hill to Rio del Mar Beach.

Shore View Cafe was a short walk down to the shoreline and must cater to people having a day on the beach. Today's chilly rain would keep most people away. Though I did see a few hardy solitary figures walking along the sand.

I parked in the small lot in front of the café. I checked my phone, hoping to see a text from Elana, but there was nothing.

A few plastic tables and chairs were stacked outside the door. Inside, the café was very small and had three or four small tables for seating. There was a small espresso machine, a menu of sandwiches posted on the wall behind the counter and clear freezer case with partially filled tubs of ice cream that looked a little worse for wear.

"What can I get you, miss?" A mustached man wearing an apron over his Hawaiian shirt came out of the back room and leaned over the counter. He looked excited to see someone actually come into his store.

"I'll have a Café Americano. Do you have any cookies?" I'd been awake almost twelve hours and was fading fast. I needed a shot of caffeine and sugar.

"We have the wafer cookies we put in with the ice cream."

"That works for me," I smiled. I pulled the photo of Nico out of my purse. "A friend of mine was here last Friday. Did you happen to see him?"

He looked at the photo and immediately nodded. "He was here. Sat at an outside table and ate sandwiches with another guy. They talked for an hour or so out there."

"Can you describe the person he was with?"

"Older guy. Around my age." The man headed for the espresso machine and began working on my Americano. I judged him to be in his fifties. "He was wearing sunglasses, so it was hard to see his eyes."

My mental database kicked in. I needed to look up Jeff Cantwell's picture. But from the description, this guy could have been Reggie McFerrin. I still didn't know what to think about Reggie, and the eviction notice Elana and I had dug up.

Was Reggie involved—or did he know somebody at the trailer park who had been involved in Nico's death?

"If you had to guess, what were they talking about? Was it like two friends getting together? A business deal?"

The man scrunched up his face as the machine began to hiss. "Well, I don't know how to answer that. I don't listen in on conversations. They didn't seem like they were friends. They weren't laughing or smiling or nothing. They talked for almost an hour."

"Okay, thanks—"

"Frank. My name's Frank." He looked at me over the top of the espresso machine, a curious look in his eyes. "Why are you asking about this guy? Ex-boyfriend?"

"Nope." I shook my head. "He was murdered last Friday. Behind my bakery in River Grove. I'm trying to figure out where he went and who he talked to that day."

Maybe it was in solidarity with me, another café owner. In a few minutes, Frank brought me over a decent Café Americano is a tall Styrofoam cup, along with a paper bag stuffed full of wafer cookies.

I had my fix. I would sit in my car munching these down and think about what to do with the information I'd gotten.

Frank waved his hand dismissively when I pulled out my wallet. "Good luck."

By the time I got back to the Laughing Loaf, it was

almost 5 p.m. I went in through the back door and glanced around the baking room with delight. The metal bread tables shone, and all dishes and utensils had been run through the dishwasher and put away. The floors were swept.

I opened the large refrigerator to see Beck had mixed the cinnamon roll dough. Two large tubs sat doing their cold rise.

Everything looked so tidy, I turned on the music. I loaded up the mixer with ingredients for brioche, singing loudly to the 1980s song by the Romantics—"That's What I Like About You."

I'd gotten some good information today. I knew what questions to ask now, and I had some people out there getting information for me.

And I had the best employee ever.

It was probably because I had the volume of the music in the back room cranked up so high. When I heard something shatter, it sounded like a bottle or glass had fallen off a shelf. I groaned, ready to get the broom out and do cleanup. Maybe the shelf with our Italian coffee flavorings bottles had collapsed.

I turned off the music.

In the distance, tires squealed angrily down the main drag.

Someone outside screamed: *Oh my God, did you see that?*

I ran to the front dining area to find the carefully tidied floor and tables covered in shards of broken glass. The front window was smashed. Glass lay on the tables, the floor, the coffee service station.

In the middle of the floor lay a large rock with the word DIE painted in black.

Chapter Fifteen

I swept up glass as Deputy Brad crouched down to examine the rock in the middle of the bakery's dining area.

I'd called my father, to let him know. And Elana, who said she was heading right over with some dinner and wine. And Beck, who told me she'd be there as soon as she could, to help with cleanup.

The chief was in San Jose for a police event, so Deputy Brad Castro ran across the street from city hall to respond to my call.

"Can you think of anyone who would do this?" Brad stood up and stepped around a large shard of glass.

I thought about my afternoon investigation and wondered if I'd touched a nerve with one of the people I'd questioned.

A group of River Grovians mostly high school students, had gathered in front of the open doorway, talking excitedly. They'd been on the sidewalk on their way to RG's Pizza when the window had been smashed. Some of the older students had gone to school with Brad, and weren't taking his authority as seriously as they would have the chief's.

"Hey, *Braaad*." One of the older guys in a plaid shirt called out to the deputy. "What are you waiting for? Get on your motorcycle and chase 'em down."

"I saw it—it was a white van," a young woman in a flannel jacket called to Brad. "A kidnapper van. You know, the kind with no windows."

"I tried to get the license plate," said a redheaded kid bearing a striking resemblance to Stewart Hamilton. "But the plates were off."

"It looked like a woman was driving," said a short, dark-haired kid with his hands in his pockets.

"Didn't look like it to me, Aiden." The young woman told Brad. Now I recognized her as the chief's granddaughter, Chloe. "More like a guy with longer hair."

Deputy Brad waved me over to a table near the back of the dining area that wasn't covered with glass shards.

"Ms. Markley, do you know of anyone who has a grudge against you?"

Aside from Nate Behrens, no. I couldn't imagine him doing this. He'd already acted against me by legal means— which had the potential to do greater damage.

Unless it was someone from my life in Seattle. I had to trust that the marshals were monitoring that, and that my father's and my identities were safe. Besides, throwing a huge rock through the front window of my business was probably not the first action a foreign government would take in retaliation for my testimony in court.

Brad sat waiting for my answer, his hands folded on the table. I'd better fess up.

"I did some—snooping around today along the coast. To

check on where Nico Behrens went on the day of his death."

Brad stared at me, frowning. "What? What do you mean—like detective work or something?"

"Yeah. My theory was, Nico Behrens might actually have stolen the cufflinks. I wanted to see if he'd tried to sell them to local jewelers."

"You can't go doing stuff like that." The deputy sat back in his chair and shook his head. With the incredulity in his voice, he sounded like he was about eighteen years old. Suddenly I felt very old.

"I want Nico's killer to be found, so I can have my bakery back." I held back a yawn; this had been a long day. And it would continue on long into the night. I'd have to figure out how to clean up this mess and cover the opening left by the smashed window. I had thousands of dollars of equipment here I needed to keep safe.

Brad stared at me like he was trying to parse what I'd just said.

"You can't go off on your own. The chief's going to be super mad about this." He wrote some notes down on his tablet. Then he looked up quickly, a curious glint in his eyes. "So, what did you find out?"

I told him about the jewelers' responses and what I learned about Jeff Cantwell—and Frank at the cafe. The deputy jotted down notes as I spoke.

"Do you think Nico had the cufflinks with him that day?"

I shook my head. "I wish I knew. He either had them on him, or he'd kept them somewhere safe while he went looking for a jeweler. Maybe some accomplice had them, here in town." My thoughts ran to his brother.

The deputy sat back in his chair and thought about this.

"Gracie, you can't investigate on your own. This is our job," he pleaded. He rubbed his face and looked out the growing number of people assembling outside. "I'm gotta do some crowd control. Why don't you give me the names of the jewelers you talked to. And, just to be safe, the café owner, too." He opened his notebook and made a list of the businesses I named.

Crowds were gathering around the open door and broken window. Then Beck came through the front door, followed by her husband, Sam, whom I'd only met when he'd dropped her off at work one morning.

Sam stood assessing the situation, then took a heavy-duty tape measurer and went to work measuring the window frame. The deputy looked concerned and approached him. Sam began gesturing and Brad nodded.

"Gracie!" Beck stared at the mess and gingerly stepped around the piles of glass I'd swept up. When she reached me, she gave me a big hug. "Who could have done this?"

"And it all looked so beautiful when I came back from Santa Cruz." I said ruefully.

Sam stepped over a pile of shards toward me. "I'll go over to the lumber yard in Boulder Creek and get some plywood to nail over the front. That should keep the place safe till you get the glass replaced."

I heard a deep growl of a voice respond from near the door.

"Need some help, neighbor? I'll join you."

"Awesome, Nate." Sam gave a thumbs up.

The bottom of my stomach dropped out. Nate stood in the doorway. He surveyed the room, a serious look in his eyes.

"I'm sorry this happened, Gracie."

I had wanted to keep Nate cast as the villain in this scenario, but he'd just messed that up.

While Brad interviewed the teen witnesses, Beck and I swept and filled cardboard boxes with broken glass. Elana showed up with a container of lasagna and a small bottle of red wine—which I put away for when I was done.

Somebody had put the word out.

My regulars, Annie Morton, and her husband Eric, joined us with push brooms they'd brought with them. Once we'd finally finished sweeping, Beck and Chloe Westerman vacuumed the floors to get tiny fragments, then wiped down the tables and seats so we could open for customers the next morning.

It was a long night.

By the time I left at 10 p.m., there were plywood panels securely nailed in place over the opening. The dining area looked as good as Beck had left it that afternoon.

I went home and I ate lasagna and drank wine directly from the little bottle Elana brought me. As I laughed and cried at the same time, I told my father about everyone who'd helped. I was wired as if I'd drunk five cups of coffee, yet my body was ready to drop.

I collapsed on my bed, Biga curled at my feet, and slept a long, deep sleep.

Chapter Sixteen

The day after the rock smashed my window, I had a nearly full house. The necessary but unsightly plywood covering on the storefront didn't seem to be dissuading anyone from coming into the bakery.

Especially not the teens before school. At 7:30, a group of teens gathered in the dining area drinking their flavored coffees, giggling, and talking. Most of them grabbed their backpacks and left for school by 8, but Chloe Westerman lingered behind while everyone left.

She approached me after I had just refilled the case with a new tray of cinnamon rolls.

"Ms. Markley?" Her face looked anxious. "Can I talk with you about something?"

"Absolutely." I said firmly and encouragingly, remembering all the adults who had made time for me as a teenager. "Let's go to the back room."

The young woman, wearing a jeans jacket and frayed and holey jeans followed me to the bread tables. Behind his gate, Biga looked up with interest. *Finally. Maybe this human will give me pets. Or food?*

Chloe looked around the room, as she fiddled with the frayed strap of her backpack. Fresh loaves of brioche lay on the cooling racks. "So, this is where you make everything. It smells so good in here."

"What's up, Chloe?" I wanted to give her time to talk, but this was our busiest time of day. The young woman swallowed, then took a deep breath.

"You know the stuff that was taken at Speed Spot?"

I nodded.

"I know who did it." She bit her lip and looked at the floor. "I found out last night. He's... a friend of a friend. He needed money. His mom's a single parent and has cancer, and he was trying to help out. Mayor C started a GoFundMe last year for them, but they already used the money they got and felt embarrassed that they needed more. He's kind of a tough kid, but it's not like he's a bad person or anything. I don't want to tell my grandpa. I can't. He'd arrest him." Her face twisted.

"And the missing laptop—that your grandfather found?"

Had this person (presumably a kid) taken the laptop, then returned it once he realized it had caused a county-wide search?

"He taped bubble wrap around it and put it in the city hall mail slot. He was really scared about what would happen to him." Chloe lowered her voice and looked around, suddenly nervous that she could be overheard.

At the meeting in the high school theatre, the chief had trumpeted the fact that the laptop had "been recovered," as if he'd hunted it down himself. He'd actually just picked it up next to the front door when he'd walked into work one morning.

"Chloe, you better get to school." The girl was watching

the long hand on the big clock inch closer to 8:15. "Let me think about this. Come in tomorrow morning, at 7 if you can – meet me at the back door in the alley and bring your friend. I have some ideas."

Chloe took a deep breath as she slid her backpack straps up over her arms. "Thank you, Ms. Markley. Please don't tell *anyone*."

"Don't worry." I assured her with a wry smile. "I'm good at keeping secrets."

And with that Chloe Westerman shot off through the door, blonde hair flying behind her, on her way down the street to the high school.

Around 10:30 a.m., things had slowed down. Without the crowd, I realized how dark the dining room had become, with half of the room's windows blocked by plywood. An older couple sat reading on their tablets in the dining room, enjoying a leisurely coffee together. Through the window in the front door, I saw the Mortons at a table outside, talking with Mayor C while their dog drank from the water bowl I set out each morning.

I was bringing out the last tray of cinnamon rolls when Chief Westerman and Brad Castro stepped up to the counter to order.

"You got some time to talk, Gracie?" The chief's face was stern. He was carrying a folder and a big yellow notepad. When Brad saw me, he shifted on his feet nervously and looked away.

I was about to get a lecture on "snooping" from the chief.

"Let me get these rolls into the case, then we can talk." I eased around Beck, who had already started on the men's coffee orders. I bent down to slide the tray into the case, then straightened up, feeling soreness in my legs from bending down sweeping glass last night.

"When you get your drinks, meet me at the corner table."

Five minutes later, the three of us gathered around the back corner table.

"I'll keep this short." The chief pulled out a notepad. "We got some information from our interviews this morning with the jewelry stores. Cliffside Jewelers has a vehicle that could be described as a 'kidnapper van' as my granddaughter calls it—and so does Frank DeCarlo at Shore View Café."

Frank hadn't seemed like a bad guy to me. I mean, he had given me cookies. Had his sympathy for me as a fellow business owner been a ploy? I did mention the name of my bakery to him. He could have easily looked it up and come back later in his van. But why? Did he have something to do with Nico's death?

"Frank DeCarlo was a suspect in a robbery in Capitola a few years ago." The chief took a big gulp of his latte, as if he especially needed the caffeine this morning. He may have been up late handling much of this last night with Brad.

"Just because he was a suspect doesn't mean he did it. What about Jeff Cantwell at Cliffside Jewelers?" I was annoyed that the chief wasn't following my line of thinking here. "He met with Nico and then went to Brussels to the diamond market. Maybe his wife or his family could have—"

The chief shook his head. "We talked to his wife. Then had a long conversation with him by phone. He's a squirrely guy, and I don't trust him farther than I can throw him. But we verified it. The trip was booked months ago. And when we talked to all the jewelers, we concluded that Mr. Behrens did not have the cufflinks on him that day."

Brad nodded. "None of them saw the cufflinks."

I had already figured this out. But if Nico hadn't had the jewels on him the day of his death, where were they? I wondered if they were on the Behrens property.

Nate may be completely unaware that his brother had hidden them there. Or worse, he could know they were there and had been in league with Nico all along. My stomach churned uncomfortably. I realized something that surprised me for a moment: I did not want this to be the case.

Yet someone had wanted those diamonds. Badly enough to get Nico out of the way to get them. Did that person have the diamonds now? Or were they still missing?

"What you did was wrong, Gracie."

Now the chief was launching into his lecture, and instinctively I cringed waiting for it. He frowned and gave me an angry look that helped me understand why Chloe Westerman had been afraid to talk to him about her friend.

"Brad told me what you did yesterday." Brad shrunk lower in his seat. "Sure, we have more information now. We know Nico Behrens didn't have the diamonds with him, and that he probably didn't have time to pass them on to anybody else. But you made somebody very angry by asking questions."

"Who was meeting with Nico at the café? If the jewelers weren't involved with his death, maybe that person was. According to Frank at the café, they talked for almost an hour." Hopefully Frank's statement had been true; the chief had quickly destroyed my trust in the café owner. "Maybe that person gave the poison to Nico."

The chief shifted in his seat, a skeptical look on his face. "Frank gave us a description—medium build, wearing sunglasses. That could be anybody. There's nothing else to identify the guy. No actual physical characteristics."

The chief was right. This person could have been masquerading as someone else—like Reggie McFerrin. I didn't know what to think of the saloon owner after Elana and I found the buried eviction notice.

"We're checking out the alibis of everyone Nico talked to on the day of his death. And for last night. We've ruled one possibility out. Cantwell was out of the country as of yesterday morning, and his wife was watching their grand-kids last night in Aptos."

"Where does that leave us?" I let out a sigh. "We're no closer to finding out who killed Nico Behrens. Or who destroyed my window."

I looked over at the plywood planks over the large front window frame. Nate and Sam had done a good job of putting it up, but I wanted my old storefront back.

"Gracie, I hope this incident has convinced you." The chief took a final gulp of coffee, and I could see his enormous Adam's apple bob as he swallowed it. "There is no 'we.' Stop your snooping. Let the police handle this."

I'm glad he didn't make me swear I wouldn't investigate further.

Because I had no intention of stopping.

Chapter Seventeen

t noon, while I was putting a load of coffee mugs and plates in the dishwasher, Beck approached me, wide-eyed.

"Gracie, I think fridge #1 died. It doesn't feel cold."

"When's the last time you took anything out?"

Beck frowned as she thought. "Maybe an hour and a half ago. It seemed to be working then."

I pulled the dishwasher closed and started it, then went over to the sleek, aluminum industrial fridge I'd bought as a refurbished display model. It wasn't making its usual hum. When I put a hand on the side, I felt nothing but slick aluminum, absolutely still. I didn't want to let any cold air out, so I didn't open the door.

Wonderful. Broken window. Broken fridge.

I would call for repair, but I suspected we'd be waiting at least a day or two for a service call. I did not need this today.

I thought fast. We were into our slow time at the bakery, but these days we never knew when that would change.

"Anyone in the dining room?"

"Kimmy Anderson and her daughter. They're eating cinnamon rolls and reading books."

"Let's move what we can to the small fridge." I glanced at the chrome-trimmed aqua "legacy" fridge that had come with the building from its burger joint days. I'd kept it because it was adorably retro. It looked quaint, but refrigerators from the 1960s were *much* smaller than modern commercial refrigerators.

Beck gave me a skeptical look. "Really?"

"We don't have many options." I said firmly. "Let's see what we can fit in it."

It took us about thirty minutes to move everything. Thankfully, I grew up playing the old video game Tetris. That's exactly what we did—with Beck running up to the front to make espresso drinks as customers came in.

Soon we had almost everything tightly wedged in, so packed that it would take a while to dig for anything we needed. I prioritized things we'd use right away: regular and alternative milks, eggs. Four pounds of butter would not fit, no matter how we tried, so we took the sticks out of their boxes and wedged them in any open spots we could find in the tiny freezer, next to the ancient ice cube trays.

There were some fruits and cheeses I wrapped up in plastic bags—we didn't need them immediately, but they needed refrigeration. I put in a quick call to RG's Pizza across the street and a block down from us. They were willing to take the bags for a few days.

When we closed the door of the aqua fridge, Beck smiled. "He's the Little Fridge that Could. He was just waiting for a chance to make a difference. He saved the day."

"Have you ever thought of writing children's books?" I laughed at Beck. "You'd be a natural at it."

After I called in a service order for the refrigerator, Beck left for the day. I was mixing dough for the next day's rolls, when I heard someone come in the front door.

I washed my hands, wiped them on a towel and popped up to the front counter.

The white-haired man with glasses didn't look familiar to me. He was at least my father's age and wore khaki pleated slacks and a sweater vest. He was almost dressed like my father. Not dressed like 99 percent of the men in River Grove, that was for sure.

"Good afternoon. What can I get for you today?"

"I'm not usually a coffee drinker." He pursed his lips and looked over the counter and display case. He scanned the drinks menu. "Why don't you give me one of your *lah-TAY* drinks. With a scone. I hear they're good."

"Right. A latte and a scone. Any special milk in your drink? Oat, coconut, soy or almond?"

This guy must not have left his house in the past ten years, because he gave me a look as if I'd just spoken to him in a foreign language.

"Just milk." He nodded, dead serious, as he took out his credit card. "The kind from a cow."

Maybe it was the stress of the past 24 hours. My insides felt jittery. I barely held back a giggle. On top of the fact that the guy pronounced *latte* as if it was some elegant French dessert.

"Got it." I managed to reply without laughing.

With some help, he slipped his card into the pay station and when his name came up on the screen, I had to hold onto the edge of the counter.

PETER J. JORDAN

"You're Peter James Jordan. The attorney."

It wasn't his fault that Nate had decided to sue me. But the anger rose in me again, despite Nate's volunteer efforts on the plywood window covering last night. Despite the fact that the man made a damn good cup of coffee and took beautiful photos of birds. Despite the fact that I always seemed aware of his presence, whenever he was in the vicinity.

"I received a notice from you last week that I was being *sued*. For Nico Behrens' fall on my back step."

The man pulled his card back, startled.

"Excuse me?" Peter Jordan's eyes grew wide behind his spectacles. "I thought that—but didn't you—"

"There is absolutely no basis for this lawsuit." I yanked a scone from the display case with a pair of tongs and slid it into a bag. "The cause of his death has been revealed as poisoning. I can show you exactly where Nico died, and you'll see that—"

"Ms. Markley." The man stopped me with his austere, stentorian voice. He put a hand on the counter and leaned toward me. "Didn't you receive a letter from my office?"

"What letter?" The noise of the espresso machine blocked out whatever he was trying to say.

As I steamed the milk, he tapped his hand on the counter, waiting impatiently for the chance to continue.

"My assistant sent you a letter on Wednesday."

I put the top on his drink and passed it across the counter to him.

"Let me check." I went back to my tiny office and looked in my inbox. There I saw a neat pile of mail that Beck must have put there. There was a bright pink post-it note on a windowed envelope from Peter James Jordan, Attorney at Law.

A note, in Beck's scrawl, said: PROBABLY IMPORTANT!!!

It had been a crazy week. I hadn't sat at my desk since the day Nate had come in to watch the video of Nico.

I brought the letter out with me to the front counter. I ripped open the envelope and pulled out the letter.

Ms. Gracie Markley:
This letter is to inform you that my client, Nathan Behrens, has withdrawn his lawsuit against you and THE LAUGHING LOAF BAKERY.

The letter was postmarked the day after Nate had watched the video at the bakery.

"He's not suing me." Tears of relief sprung up in my eyes. I hated that I was crying in front of this guy.

Peter James Jordan calmly sipped his *lah-TAY*, as he watched me with a curious look.

"He came into my office and told me he wanted to drop the suit. Out of the blue. He said after the poisoning was confirmed that it didn't make any sense to continue with it."

I suddenly felt the weight of what I'd been carrying for the past week. I'd been scared. Even though I knew I wasn't negligent, the threat of the suit loomed over me, ready to fall and wipe out everything I'd established in River Grove.

"Thank you." I stammered. "Thank you for letting me know, Mr. Jordan."

"I advise you to check your mail more often," he said before he ate that last chunk of his scone. "This scone is very good."

After the attorney left, I locked up the front and back

doors. I'd close an hour early today, something I'd never done before.

Then I went into my office and put my head down on the desk for about an hour. On that hard oak desktop, I slept.

The sleep of the relieved.

* * *

The next morning, I came in at 5 a.m. to mix up and proof the cinnamon roll dough, since I hadn't had the fridge space to let it rise overnight. No Biga today; my dog was sleeping on my dad's bed, dreaming sweet dog dreams, and I didn't have the heart to wake him.

True, the Little Fridge that Could *had* saved the day, but it still wouldn't accommodate the large tubs of dough for the bakery's most popular item. I'd do a regular warm rise in the proofer—more work this morning, but they would taste just as good.

Chloe Westerman would be at the back door at 7, along with her friend. Everything would be ready for Beck to start on at 7:30 a.m., so I could take a few minutes to talk with them both and set up our plan.

At 6:45, as sunlight slowly filtered in through the remaining window in the dining room, I had everything in place. I started up the espresso machine and made myself an Americano.

Suddenly, a loud clanging noise rattled the dining area. It sounded like a cross between a chainsaw and the alarm on a bank vault. Laughing Loaf had an alarm system, but I'd tested it and it did not sound like this.

Someone was screaming next door at Loudon's Antique Emporium.

It sounded like Robert Loudon, arguing loudly with someone.

"You have no right to do this! Get off my property, or I'll call the police."

"You want me to call the police?" The sarcastic voice sounded like an older woman. "You'll be in a lot more trouble when the police find out what *you* did."

Then a scream—and a loud bang from inside the Antiques Emporium.

My first instinct was to run outside to the back of the antique store and see what was going on. Chloe and her friend were due at my back step any minute. I hoped and prayed they were running late and that they'd be safe.

When I ran out the back step of the bakery, I saw a blur of white. A van. With a screech, the vehicle veered toward me. Strangely, my body seemed to know what to do, and I scrambled into the thin niche between the two old buildings.

Unfortunately, when I turned to look back, I banged my knee hard on a vent jutting out of the bakery side.

The van pulled back and sped off down the alley. Pain made me cry out as I tried to put weight on my battered knee.

A minute later, another car with a swirling red light attached haphazardly to its roof roared down the alley and came to a halt in a cloud of dust by my back step.

It was Chief Westerman.

Chapter Eighteen

I limped out to the chief's car, shouting hoarsely into the open passenger seat window.

"The white van! It was next door when Loudon's alarm went off. It just went down the alley. Probably heading for the highway—"

Chief Westerman nodded, barked something into his radio, and screeched down the alley in pursuit.

I stumbled up the step, my knee hurting as if it had been whacked with a hammer. I slowly made my way into the back room and headed for the Little Fridge that Could. I pawed through butter sticks till I found the ice cube trays. I staggered to the prep table and dumped the ice cubes into a freezer bag and sat down on a stool, pressing the bag to my knee.

Of course, as soon as I started to feel relief, there was a knock at the back door. I gingerly slid down from the stool and made my way to the door.

"Come in Chloe and—you're Aiden, right?" I recognized Aiden from the glass clean-up two nights ago. The short, dark-haired kid stood behind Chloe, looking very nervous. His hands were plunged into the pockets of his jeans and his hair nearly covered his eyes, as if he were hoping to remain invisible. I smiled and led them to the back room.

I nodded at Chloe. "You just missed your grandfather. The white van came down the alley and he's chasing it right now."

"Oh, my *God*," Chloe whispered, a look of fear in her eyes. "He was just here?"

I looked at the back room clock. "I've got fifteen minutes before Beck comes in for the day, so let's make this quick. I'm talking to Jake Daniels this afternoon. He's shorthanded at Speed Spot now that his son has gone back to school. He needs help in the office, taking calls and managing the lot. It might be possible for you to work off what you stole."

"Then, like—it wouldn't go on my record?" The young man's mouth twitched.

"That is up to Chief Westerman." His face fell as soon as I said it. "After I talk to Mr. Daniels, the three of us will go in to meet with him. I know it's scary. What you did was wrong, and I think you know that. But you returned the laptop. You've got that in your favor."

"I sold the catalytic converter, though." Aiden looked down at his lap, discouraged. "A guy—one of my dad's buddies down in Gilroy—showed me how to do it. I knew it was wrong. My mom's been out of a job for six months. The landlord's been pretty nice, but if we didn't pay the rent this month, he was kicking us out. I panicked. I couldn't think of what else to do."

"Wait a minute." I thought of Elana's and my treasure hunt by The Riverside. "Do you live in the River Grove trailer park off the highway?"

Aiden nodded. "Yeah, we do. Why?"

I had no doubt Reggie McFerrin had found that notice. Maybe it had fallen out of Aiden's pocket when he'd been climbing the fence at Speed Spot the night of the burglary. It's possible with Reggie's late hours at The Riverside, he'd passed by not long after Aiden had been in the motors works yard. Maybe he'd known Aiden's situation. The ways of River Grove's legendary music hall owner were still a mystery to me.

"Aiden, I think someone had your back that night." I told him about finding the buried notice.

"What the—" Aiden looked at me, in awe. "I knew I had it with me, but then I couldn't find it anywhere."

I'd need to convince Jake Daniels that my plan would work. Any kid who knew what a catalytic converter was and how to remove it from a car probably had enough knowledge to work an entry level job at a mechanics shop—for long enough to pay off what he'd stolen. It would be a risk for Jake, but unlike my tech-spy husband, Aiden knew what he'd done was wrong and seemed willing to make amends.

"Chloe, give me your contact info, and I'll text you after I talk to Mr. Daniels." Chloe scrawled her number on a piece of notebook paper and passed it to me.

"Thanks, Gracie." She looked scared, and I didn't blame her. I didn't know what the chief would say to this plan.

Then she looked down and I saw concern growing on her face. "Gracie—your leg looks kind of weird—"

I looked down at my knee, poking out from under my skirt. It had swollen to the size of a big fat grapefruit and had a deep gash in it. Though it hurt, I had so many other things on my mind right now, that I mentally assigned it a lower priority. I'd go back to icing it when things calmed down.

"Listen, my assistant's coming in soon—and your grandfather will be back. You need to leave now. Go through the front door." I eased myself off the stool and led them haltingly to the front door. The two shouldered their backpacks and hurried down the street.

In the distance, I heard the wail of a siren coming in our direction.

When I made my way to the front counter, I saw Robert Loudon's car parked on the street in front of his shop. I hadn't noticed his car there before. He usually parked in the alley like I did.

Maybe he'd rushed to the shop, after hearing about the alarm.

As I made my way slowly to the back room to put ice on my knee, my thoughts cleared. I examined events of this morning. Loudon's alarm was triggered, and he'd had a nasty argument with someone. A woman, it sounded like.

Had the person in the white van broken into Loudon's?

I glanced at the clock and noticed it was 7:40. Beck wasn't here yet. Beck was never late. I grabbed my phone to call her.

Then I heard the sirens wail, as emergency vehicles pulled up in the alley and in front on the street.

A sick feeling in the pit of my stomach completely overshadowed the pain in my knee.

My thoughts flipped through the database of all the people I cared about in River Grove.

Chapter Nineteen

Five minutes later, to my relief, somebody pounded on the front door.

When I unlocked the door, Beck almost fell in, breathless.

"The chief and Brad just told me—oh, it's awful, Gracie. They've blocked off the alley, so I couldn't get in. I can't believe it. He's not dead, but they've rushed him to the hospital in Santa Cruz and they're not sure he'll make it."

"Who, Beck? Tell me."

She wiped her eyes. "Robert Loudon, next door. He was found in the back of his store—shot in the chest. Somebody broke in."

"I was here when the alarm went off," I said, feeling shock but also, guiltily, some relief that Beck was unharmed. "He was arguing with someone. Then the white van roared down the alley—maybe the white van of the person who broke the window. The van nearly ran me down. The chief took off after him."

It could be that the person in the van was trying to rob Robert Loudon's store, but—why? Loudon's Antiques

Emporium didn't have anything that expensive in it, as far as I knew. Last time I'd walked through the shop, I saw a few busts, some small sculptures, bad paintings, dusty glass tumblers, and colored glass pitchers that looked like they'd come from someone's grandma's house.

Nate said Nico had met with Loudon. Maybe Nico had given Loudon the cufflinks, and he'd hidden them somewhere in the shop.

Now somebody—maybe one of the people I'd talked to yesterday—knew they were there.

With the alley blocked and my swollen knee, I wasn't going anywhere. I doubted that the usual customers would be coming in this morning.

Still, I opened the bakery relatively on time and with Beck's help, we had fresh cinnamon rolls, muffins, and scones in the display case.

As I served the small stream of customers this morning, and tried to stay off my leg, I couldn't think of much else, other than where the jewels could be.

And who'd shot Robert Loudon.

In the midst of this crisis, the rhythm of bakery work seemed to have calmed Beck down. She moved easily between serving customers, working the espresso machine, and replenishing the display case—all with her usual cheeriness. At 9:30 a.m., when we were down to one customer every five minutes, she asked if she could take drinks and baked goods over to the detectives working at Loudon's shop. I saw Brad's car and the chief's, as well as a couple of cars from Santa Cruz PD parked in front.

"You can't get up while I'm gone, Gracie." Beck commanded with a new authority. "Stay off your knee, behind the counter, till I get back. Promise?"

"I promise." I smiled at my assistant, and she began

filling bags with rolls and scones. I set up a boxed cardboard carrier for drip machine coffee and filled a paper bag with creamer pods, stirrers, and napkins.

Beck loaded a box with all the items.

"I'll be back in just a few, Gracie."

I settled myself onto a stool behind the counter and pressed the ice bag onto my knee. After the rush and noise of the morning, everything seemed eerily quiet. A wave of loneliness and sadness passed over me. I missed Biga's presence, but there was no way I could hobble home and get him today. Even if his tail-wagging cheeriness and unconditional love were what I needed now.

I called my father and told him I wouldn't be home till later, and I might need a ride. I told him to give Biga pets and kisses for me.

When the bell tinkled at the door, I half rose off my stool, ready to serve customers.

I switched on the espresso machine, then looked up to see Nate Behrens. He had his camera around his neck and was wearing his outdoorsman outfit—sturdy cargo pants with a grey sweater that hugged his chest. My stomach started that weird fluttering thing again.

"I was heading out for a shoot over in Bonny Doon, when I heard the news about Loudon." He turned his blue eyes on me, but this time I didn't feel that uncomfortable, bug-under-the-magnifying-glass feeling. There was something different about this look.

"Are you okay, Gracie?"

I swallowed, not quite sure how to interact with him in this new way. I blurted out my story like a six-year-old running to their mother after a bad playground injury.

"I-I went outside because Loudon and some woman

were yelling, and then a van tried to run me down. I ran in between the two buildings and bashed my knee against a vent and—"

He frowned then demanded in his deep voice: "Let me see it." He came around the counter and bent down to look at the knee. "Good that you're icing it." He went and got a padded stool in the seating area and set it down in front of me. He lifted my leg onto it to elevate it. I was surprised, maybe shocked, but I let him do it.

"How badly does it hurt?"

"Maybe a seven or eight—on a scale of ten," I responded.

"Okay if I check your freezer?"

I nodded, curious about his request. Then remembering, I shouted out the warning as he went into the back room. "It's the little aqua fridge. But be careful—it's full of butter."

Thank God the service person was coming at 2:30 p.m.

In a few minutes Nate came back with a big bag of frozen blueberries.

"Let's see if this works better." His large hands molded the bag of frozen berries around my knee. The direct contact of coolness instantly made my knee feel better. Then Nate bent down and zipped opened his backpack. He pulled out a roll of elastic bandage. He wrapped it around to hold the bag in place. It looked goofy. I looked like I'd been in a bad fight in the freezer aisle of the grocery story.

"Feels great." I sighed. "But it looks a little ridiculous."

He looked at me, the corners of his mouth turning up. "I'm thinking you'd prefer relief over fashion right now."

"You'd be right."

"Are you able to leave? You should have that looked at.

That scrape looks pretty deep; it could get infected. Let me drive you down to the ER in Santa Cruz."

"When Beck gets back from taking coffee to the team next door. Then I have to be back by 2:30 for the fridge guy."

Oh, geez. I also promised to talk to Jake Daniels about Aiden.

"Beck could let the service man in." He gave me a sideways look that I read as: *She can handle this, and you have trust issues.* I could have been projecting a little.

Beck got back ten minutes later, with the news that the chief hadn't been able to catch the white van.

"He said there's a bulletin out for the van. The guy who did this is still out there," a cloud passed over her normally cheery face. "That's scary, especially if he was the person broke our window."

Beck looked from Nate to me with a puzzled look on her face.

"Is everything okay?" she asked timidly, knowing that the last time I'd spoken about Nate it had been in a *very* angry voice.

Nate and I answered in unison:

> "He's taking me to the ER."
> "I'm taking her to the ER."

Beck raised her eyebrows and looked at me with a faint smile. "Okay, then."

Nate helped me up and out the front door to his car. At one point, he carried me over the curb in his arms, to avoid me having to navigate the mangled curb, still cracked from the 1989 Loma Prieta quake. Nobody had carried me that way before. I felt like a Jane Austen heroine.

All of this was dizzying for me. Now that we were together in his car, I remembered what I'd wanted to ask him earlier today.

"Can I ask you—Did Nico know Robert Loudon?"

He glanced across at me. "He was going to meet with him. At some restaurant on the coast."

I spilled out my thoughts—the investigative trip I'd taken down to Santa Cruz, the jewelers I'd talked to and the feeling I'd gotten that Robert Loudon was involved in Nico's death. There was a connection there. I knew it, but I couldn't pin down the details.

"Nate, I think Nico stole the cufflinks. He may have left them with someone in River Grove."

Nate let out a deep sigh. He shook his head as we drove out in sight of the coast with its grey clouds and empty, drab-looking beach.

I was getting text after text from Elana, wondering if I was okay after today's shooting next door. I sent her a quick response: *I'm fine. TTYL.* Then silenced my phone.

"I came to the same conclusion. He wouldn't talk to me about it." He pulled onto Highway 1 as the sun cut through the thick grey cloud cover. "I raised him, so he always thought of me as a nagging parent. He made sure they weren't in the house where I could find them."

"I believe he gave them to Robert Loudon to keep them safe. And maybe that was a bad idea."

"Do you think—" Nate started to talk, his voice hoarse. "That Loudon killed Nico? Maybe Loudon didn't want to give Nico back the cufflinks. I heard rumors that his business was failing. The store that his great grandfather started. Three hundred and fifty thousand dollars would help keep his shop open. He wouldn't be the one responsible for running the family business into the ground."

Nate became quiet for a while. It wasn't an uncomfortable silence. He looked deep in thought, processing his brother's actions.

Finally, we got off the freeway and turned onto a side street.

"I wanted to believe he didn't do it. That he'd turned his life around." Nate said quietly. "But he was like this growing up. When he saw something he liked, he took it. As his guardian, I felt like a failure. I do now."

I had a hard time agreeing with this, from what I'd heard him say in his talk at the theatre. He'd done all he could. I wanted to add that Nico's ability to evade the law put him in criminal mastermind territory, but I knew that wouldn't be helpful right now.

When we got to the parking lot for the ER, Nate came around to my side and lifted me to my feet, then supported me as we walked in.

He leaned into me as we walked and spoke low into my ear. "I am sorry for the suit. That was wrong. It had nothing to do with you, Gracie."

* * *

Two hours later, I walked out of the ER on Nate's arm, with a cleaned, stitched wound, a cool new bandage, and an appointment for an MRI next week for a suspected torn meniscus.

Nate wanted to drop me off at home, where I could keep my knee elevated, but I told him to take me back to The Laughing Loaf. I wanted to be there for the fridge repair person, to hear the damage. I suspected it would be expensive. And I still needed to talk to Jake Daniels.

Reluctantly, he helped me inside the bakery. Beck had

left for the day, after another amazing tidying job, judging by the gleaming surfaces and spotless floor. I had a lot of worries in my life today. Having a bad assistant wasn't one of them.

"You were right to insist that I get my knee looked at." I felt uncomfortable and oddly shy. "And thanks for your help with boarding up the window the other night."

He smiled. "You told me last week that River Grove was all about the community. People helping other people. I got a lot of meals and dinner invites after my talk at the high school. I was doing my part to pay back."

After he left, I put my head down on the counter and did a weird combination of laughing and crying.

The fridge repairman didn't take long to assess the issue in my refurbished fridge.

"It's the fan motor, *ma'am*." I flinched as he stuck that last word on his sentence. "It needs to be replaced. The good news is I know I can pick one up in Santa Cruz. I'll be back in an hour." The repairman left his toolbox, which I took as a sign that he'd come back.

I called Jake Daniels and asked if he could meet me at the bakery instead. I told him I had an idea I'd like to run past him, and it concerned the break-in at his lot. He told me he come over after he closed at 4.

The repairman wasn't back by the time Jake got there. I hobbled over to the door and let him in, and we sat at a table in the dining room.

"I had somebody come to the bakery today. A teenage boy. He confessed to breaking into Speed Spot's lot and stealing the converter and the laptop."

"Has there been an arrest?" Jake put his fist down on the table. "I can't believe the chief didn't find this out—"

"Jake." I put my hand on the table between us. "This is

a *kid*. A scared teenager who needed money to help his mom pay rent. He panicked. He regrets it, and he turned the laptop over to the police. He's willing to make amends for the catalytic converter."

Jake looked skeptical. "What are you proposing, Gracie?"

"This kid knows his way around cars. He's willing to work hard. You're shorthanded since Kai went back to school."

Jake crossed his arms and looked even more skeptical, and I wondered if my do-good mentality had gone a little too far. Was I in touch with reality at this point?

"What if you have this kid work off the debt at Speed Spot?"

"I don't know this kid. How can I trust him?" Jake threw up his hands. "He stole from me. From my *customers*."

"I know it's a risk, but maybe this is the second chance he needs. With everyone you hire, you take a risk. Beck had no experience except babysitting. Bringing her on at Laughing Loaf has been one of the best decisions I've ever made. You could change this young man's life."

Jake leaned back in the chair, arms still crossed.

"Let me meet him," he said gruffly. "Then I'll decide. I'm not thrilled with this scenario."

I nodded. "That's fair, Jake. Let's arrange a meetup. How about he comes over when you close Speed Spot tomorrow—at 4 p.m.?"

As the repairman returned and headed for the back room, Jake agreed to at least talk to Aiden. Once I had an agreement with him, I'd approach the chief—hopefully with Chloe, and Aiden himself.

I hoped this worked out. What a strange day it had been.

I would find out in the next half hour, after the repairman and Jake left, it was by no means over.

Chapter Twenty

It was 5 p.m. and I felt the growing cold outside.

The pink sky slowly faded until all light was snuffed out. The dining room looked especially dark and gloomy with the plywood covering.

But my fridge was back in action. I'd mix bread dough for an overnight rise and roll out laminated scones for freezing.

Normally I was home by this time, preparing dinner. Tomorrow was another day, and I still needed to finish prep for my bakes.

I checked in with my dad, who told me not to worry about making dinner for him. Mary Jo Hartman had invited him out for steak.

I wished I was home, cuddling with Biga on the couch and watching a good mystery on Brit Box. Beck had offered to come in to help, but I told her I'd be able to handle everything. It just might take me longer than usual.

Around 5:15 Elana called. It was good to hear her voice.

"What is going on with your knee, girl? And Robert Loudon? I heard he's in the hospital and may not make it."

"I'm sorry I didn't call you back. Everything happened today. I'm serious. *Everything*."

I told her about my day, and what had happened at Loudon's, and the white van. And my trip to the ER with Nate Behrens.

"Is there something going on between you guys?" She asked.

"Of course not," I said firmly.

"Hmmm," Elana said, with some skepticism.

"Nate was being nice. He's sorry he tried to sue me."

"Okaaay," said Elana, the loyal friend. "I still think that was a jerk move on his part. 'Sorry' isn't going to make it all better. At least not for me."

I gave her as much of an update on the Aiden issue as I could without identifying him.

"Oh, and the eviction notice we found on our treasure hunt? I found out who it belongs to. I believe Reggie McFerrin buried it to protect the kid who broke into Speed Spot. He thinks it fell out of his pocket when he scaled the fence."

"So at least one mystery is solved. I can see Reggie wanting to help a kid like that." Elana's voice was soft with affection. "He's such a nice guy."

I mentally threw up my hands. What was it about Reggie McFerrin? Again, it must take a River Grove long-timer to appreciate The Riverside's quirky owner. I was obviously missing something.

"Let me pick you up tonight, Gracie. You shouldn't be driving with that knee."

I was filled with relief. She was right; I shouldn't.

"Oh, God—thank you. Does 7 p.m. work?"

"Of course. See you then, Gracie."

I went back to my biga loaves, shaping the boules from

the bulk fermentation tub that had been sitting in the proofer. The dough smelled rich, with a slight scent of wine. I floured the bannetons and filled them with dough balls, then set them in the proofer.

The room grew darker and colder as I worked. I wanted to turn on the music system and play some upbeat 80s tunes, maybe some good old Wham!, but with my knee it would be hard to reach up to the shelf on tiptoe to turn on the music system.

As I was rolling out dough for the scones, I heard sounds in the alley. Car tires rolling over gravel. Soon, thumping noises in Loudon's next door.The police could be doing a search of the place again.

Nate had used a large portion of my blueberries on my knee today, but after rummaging through my cupboards I found dried cranberries and then grated some orange zest. After folding them into the dough, and making several turns and folds, I had my slabs to cut. I took my knife, Andúril, and made neat, diagonal slices in the dough to form triangles, then placed the scones on trays, and wrapped them for baking tomorrow morning. Satisfied, I slid them into the roomy freezer of my now-operational, full-size fridge.

Noises continued next door. Were they doing some kind of crime scene clean-up?

I went to the back door of the bakery to see if I could catch a glimpse of what was going on at Loudon's. The light was bad in the alley. I didn't see any police cruisers. I resolved that when all of this was over, I'd have decent lighting installed at the back of the bakery.

I opened the door and as quietly as I could, moved toward the back of Loudon's brick building, toward the multi-paned windows.

A light bounced inside the shop, as if someone was

going through with a flashlight. I heard voices but couldn't make out what they were saying. Whoever was inside wasn't trying to keep quiet. But then apart from The Riverside, River Grove's downtown shut down at 6 p.m. I rarely stayed at the bakery this late. There was nobody around.

I could picture Loudon poisoning Nico in order to keep the cufflinks to himself. But what if Loudon was working with one of the jewelers I'd talked to—to have the diamonds cut or reset? Loudon must have had a partner. That could explain the person in the van, trying to scare me off the trail and then trying to break into Loudon's to look for the goods.

They'd likely shot Loudon, who probably had no intention of handing over the cufflinks.

I looked around for options. I could move along the other side of the building to get closer. I wanted to see who it was. Hear what they were saying.

Moving slowly, because my knee gave me no choice, I stayed low and in the shadows till I was near the far corner of Loudon's Antique Emporium.

I'd started to edge around the corner when I heard someone breathing heavily behind me.

And felt a sharp jab in my back.

"Miss Markley. Nice to see you again." It was a woman's voice. I turned around to see Rosamond Steele, holding a handgun.

"Wonderful. You got here just in time to help us."

Chapter Twenty-One

Rosamond prodded me up the steps into the back door of Loudon's shop. I hobbled slowly, winching with knee pain. Judging by the consistent jabs at my back, Rosamond was losing patience with my speed.

"The police disabled the alarm when they were here this morning." She smirked at her daughter, who stood inside the door with a flashlight. "The police are always so helpful."

"You know what we're looking for, Gracie." Ray Steele said, clutching the flashlight. "Bob Loudon thought he could cut us out. He made us a deal. We'd help him reset the diamonds for resale, then we'd get half the proceeds when they were sold. After he poisoned the underwear model, he decided to keep them. What were we supposed to say to Loudon? 'Show us these incredible diamonds, then feel free to renege on the deal? Go ahead, Bob. Do what works for *you*.'"

"When it was obvious he wasn't going to share, I shot

him." Rosamond looked pleased with her simple solution to the problem.

"We have you to thank, Gracie," Ray said with a twist in her voice. "After you came by, we realized the diamonds came from the LA photo shoot. We looked up the details. Loudon told us they were worth only a quarter of that. After we talked to you, we knew what a liar he was."

"We're sure the cufflinks are here," Rosamond said from behind me, a sharp tone in her voice. "And you're going to help us look, Gracie. Once we find them, we're out of here. We've got tickets for an overnight flight to Brussels."

We made our way down the dark hall to the front of the store, a jumble of tables and cabinets displaying knick-knacks and dusty, worthless items of the quality you'd find at a garage sale. With the exception of two, exquisite cufflinks featuring ten-carat diamonds.

"When you try to sell them in Brussels, everyone will know where they came from. You'll be arrested." I limped, trying to keep pressure off my leg. I tried to think of any way to let the outside world know where I was. Elana would be looking for me soon.

"Not your problem right now, honey. You just find the cufflinks, and maybe we'll let you live." Rosamond sounded almost motherly as she continued to jab the end of the gun into my back.

We started at the front of the store. Ray opened jewelry boxes and antique Chinese cabinets—anything that looked expensive. I went for cheaper items that Bob Loudon might think would be overlooked: tacky ceramic cat jewelry dishes, old colored glass bottles, a creepy doll with anguished eyes holding a wicker basket. Nothing.

We lifted tables and looked up underneath their legs to

see if anything was taped to them. We searched the pockets of all the vintage dresses and coats hanging on a rack.

What time is it? There were clocks everywhere. Clocks on the walls, the tables, the shelves. None of them seemed set to the correct time. Elana said she was coming by at 7. If I wasn't at the bakery, she'd suspect something was up. I glanced to see a huge bear head, mounted above the front window of the store. Suddenly I had a thought.

"Up there, by the bear!" I called out. "I saw something sparkle."

Ray quickly turned the flashlight on the window, shining it across the front until she moved it upward, onto the bear.

Rosamond grunted in disgust. "I don't see a thing."

I willed Elana, my father, the Chief, Brad, anyone outside—to notice the light.

Now Ray shone the flashlight on a nearby table devoted to figurines and statues. A couple of them looked like awards. One was a bowling trophy from 1962.

I spotted a small bust about a foot high with a green patina on it—of a man with a beard and sideburns looking off into the distance, with what looked like a border of logs etched into the base. I bent down to read the plaque attached to it.

Samuel Hezekiah Loudon (1853-1925)

Loudon's great grandfather, founder of the original Loudon's Emporium. My heart pounded with excitement. If Loudon had killed Nico and taken the diamonds in order to keep the Loudon legacy alive, this could be it.

Rosamond poked my back with the gun. "Who cares about a damn statue."

I picked up the bust. "Hold on—this could be it."

I lifted it and turned it over. The sculpture was hollow and there was a hole in the bottom. I shook it and heard a faint rattle.

Ray pulled the bust from my hands. Rosamond watched eagerly as Ray dug a finger into the hole and pulled out a tissue-wrapped bundle.

Rosamond gasped. Ray took a deep breath and carefully cleared a spot on the table.

She gently laid the bundle down to open it. Lying there were two stunning cufflinks, huge beveled rectangular diamonds in a modern silver setting. I've heard people rave about diamonds and how beautiful they are. I never understood what they saw in them.

These diamonds were crystal clear, perfectly unblemished, gleaming under the flashlight's beam like the San Luciano River in the noonday sun. I couldn't take my eyes off them.

I knew why Nico took them. As Nate had said, Nico took things he liked, and these were beyond a doubt, beautiful. Nico wouldn't keep them at home with his brother. Nate would, of course, make him give them back.

In the distance, sirens began their windup. I could hear them faintly. Relief washed over me; the light had been seen. Ray and Rosamond seemed unaware, transfixed by what they'd just found. They commented to each other on the stones' clarity.

The women watched the jewels glisten in the beam of the flashlight, mesmerized. Everyone has their drug, I guess. Diamonds are beautiful, but they're not my drug.

"Police," Rosamond croaked hoarsely, and the two women stared at each other, before Ray scooped up the cufflinks and slid them into her pocket.

The women ran to the back exit, slamming the door behind them as they headed for the alley. I heard the crunch of car tires wheeling back in the gravel. Then the chief on the bullhorn, calling for Ray and Rosamond to surrender.

In a few minutes, after the bullhorn stopped, I heard the scratch of voices on the police radio. The Steeles had been arrested. I stumbled toward the back door in the dark, and when I opened it, Elana was right there.

She hugged me so tightly it hurt.

After what seemed like hours of answering questions, I was free to lock up at The Laughing Loaf and go home.

Elana stayed with me till I was finished, then we sat in my kitchen while I filled her in on what had happened that day. We agreed that today's events, plus the finding of the missing cufflinks and Nico's killer, merited an emergency bottle of wine.

Chapter Twenty-Two

It was the first week of March.

Beck was now making her beignets as a special menu item: BECK'S BEIGNETS. She came in at 5 a.m., when I did, so she could get them cut and fried. With her earlier start time, she was also able to help me with my duties in the baking room as my knee recovered.

This morning, smells of the sweet fried treats filled the bakery. By 7:20 a.m., Beck had filled a tray with lightly browned beignets and was topping them with dollops of honey and a dusting of powdered sugar before she took them out to the display case.

The fried dough pillows looked and smelled like fluffy bits of heaven. On our test run a few days ago, they sold out fast. Last night, Elana texted me to put some aside for her, since Kirk had gotten some on the way to work the other day and couldn't stop talking about them. Beck glowed with confidence at the positive response to her work and told me with a mysterious look that she was testing out a new, filled version at home.

Mayor C and the chief had also started coming in to the bakery earlier, to hold their daily meeting at the corner table, or outside if it was sunny, with their coffee and beignets.

Today the two were second in line, behind Jake Daniels. They put in their order and stood chatting amiably with Beck and I.

"What do you two talk about in your meetings now that there's no more crime in River Grove?" I asked innocently, as I passed them their plate of warm beignets.

The chief already had a beignet in hand, and his latte wasn't even ready yet.

"We've got to prepare for the next one. Right, Corinne?" He winked at the mayor, who wisely grabbed the plate with the remaining beignet out of his hands.

"You can't be too careful," Mayor C said, frowning. "The world is changing and so is River Grove. We need to keep in touch with the times and keep this a safe community. I don't want to be caught off guard again."

I smiled as the two picked up their lattes and began an intense discussion about traffic signs, in their own world as they walked out the front entrance to find a table in the sun.

At 12:30, I left Beck in charge and took a very excited Biga for a walk along the river. The doctor had given me permission to walk short distances, as long as it was on unpaved ground. My dog strained on the leash, rushing over to sniff every bush and tree stump on the way. You would have thought he'd drunk a gallon of water this morning.

The sun filtering down through the trees sparkled on the moving river. The air smelled like spring, though it was still a few weeks away. New birds had come out with the warmer weather, including a small one with an incredibly cheerful whistle that Nate told me was the Pacific Wren.

It had only been three weeks since Nico's murder, but I felt a burden lift in the past week. I could walk without much pain. Robert Loudon, Nico's killer, was expected to make a full recovery after all. The diamond-obsessed Ray and Rosamond Steele were behind bars. Aiden Franzi might possibly work for Jake Daniels at the place he robbed. I'd find out in a few days if the chief would accept this plan.

Biga and I reached the area just past The Riverside, where the path veers away from downtown and you're suddenly among the redwoods. It's not far from town, but all you can see is forest and river, and it feels like another world. The canopy of the redwoods made everything look darker and lusher, and the air smelled of damp earth and pine needles.

After I pulled Biga away from what must have been his twentieth bush, I was startled to see someone sitting on a fallen log up ahead.

I saw the sunglasses and ponytail and knew who it was immediately. He wore his usual black shirt and jeans, which seemed out of place on a bright day like today. But it was his uniform.

"Gracie Markley," he called out, with a smile.

I wanted to ask him questions. Was I the only one intimidated by him? Why did he hide his eyes behind sunglasses, even when he was inside?

I sat down on the log next to him. Biga went up to Reggie and began rubbing his nose against his legs.

"Reggie, can I ask you something?" I turned to him as Biga jumped up onto his lap. "You buried something by the river a few weeks ago. Did you know whose it was?"

The man remained quiet for a while, stroking the dog's back. Biga was very happy.

"I found it by the gate at Speed Spot and I had a feeling.

There are crimes of greed and crimes of desperation. I knew the theft was an act of desperation."

There was a difference. I thought about how those terms would apply to Robert Loudon, who'd murdered Nico. And the Steeles.

"The good news is that the kid, Aiden, may end up working at Speed Spot now. And his mom is starting to get some help." I'd heard today that a fund had been set up at the local bank for Ana Franzi.

Reggie smiled and looked down at Biga. "Perfect."

After a few minutes, he set Biga down on the ground and stood up.

"I want to show you something, Gracie."

He walked a few feet away toward a large redwood tree. Its trunk looked completely black, scarred by a recent fire. By all signs, the tree could not be alive.

"There was a fire here. The year before last, before you moved to town." He ran his hand along the charred bark. "This tree is around a hundred years old. After the fire, everyone thought the tree was dead." He stepped back, and I saw a ring of tiny green trees a few feet from the trunk. They circled the blackened tree.

"This is called a fairy ring," he said, as he stepped back farther and farther from the tree and pointed at the ground. "You can't see it, but the roots of the redwood tree stretch out far, about a hundred feet. And the other redwood trees stretch out, too. There is a whole system of roots under our feet right now. The tree might look dead or in trouble, but the roots are alive. Those roots and the roots of the other trees work together to bring new life. New little redwoods."

For some reason, I started crying. This vampire hippie had just explained River Grove to me. The town was rooted together in ways I couldn't always see. But I'd seen life from these roots. When I'd come to town after my life fell apart in Seattle and found new friends and community. When the Steeles had smashed the window of the bakery, and my friends and customers came to help and clean up. When it looked like Aiden would get a second chance and his mom some help.

"I needed to hear this today." I gave him a hug. He smelled like sandalwood incense. "Thank you."

✳ ✳ ✳

Two days later, we sat in the chief's office at city hall—me, Jake Daniels, Mayor C, Chloe, and Aiden.

"What you did was wrong in every way, young man," Chief Westerman gave Aiden Franzi a stern look. "In no way will I excuse the fact that you broke the law. You stole a laptop, and you stole valuable parts from Mr. Daniels' customers' cars."

Mayor C joined in, her face pink with emotion.

"You had a whole company frantic that valuable information had been released to the world."

Aiden sat up in his chair and swallowed hard. Chloe put a hand on the boy's shoulder. He looked like a tiny stockbroker today, in a navy suit, his hair slicked back so it no longer fell over his eyes. I'm sure Chloe had carefully chosen his look for this meeting with the chief.

"I don't expect it to be excused, sir. I take responsibility for what I did. I got scared because I thought my mom and I were going to get kicked out of our trailer. We had nowhere to go. But if I can pay for what I did by working for Mr. Daniels, I'll be very thankful."

Jake Daniels reached out and shook Aiden's hand with one of those firm, manly grips that both of them seemed to understand.

"We'll see how this goes, Aiden." Jake said sternly. "But from the time I've spent with you this week, I think there's a chance this could work."

I was in a good mood, possibly enhanced by the pain killers I was still taking. I hugged everybody, wiped a few tears from my eyes, then walked back across the street, where my father and Biga sat at a table in front of The Laughing Loaf. Beck was inside, working till closing, happy for the extra hours.

As soon as I sat down at the table, Biga jumped up on my lap and started rubbing his nose on me. He rolled over and demanded a belly rub, which I gladly gave him.

My father took a sip of his latte. "Robert Loudon's doing very well, even though he's under arrest at the hospital for Nico's murder, of course. Mary Jo heard the tetrodotoxin came from his mother, who had been a cancer patient. It's sometimes used for pain management."

"And Ray and Rosamond are in the county jail," I said as I rubbed Biga's belly. "I want someone to look at me like those women looked at those cufflinks. You should have seen their eyes when they saw those diamonds."

I laughed, and Biga seemed to think I was laughing in delight at him. He nuzzled me closer.

"You just might have that." My dad said with a playful smile.

Nate Behrens approached on the sidewalk, camera around his neck. He wore hiking shorts and a t-shirt since it was a sunny day. When he saw me, a silly grin appeared on his face.

I immediately felt my cheeks turn bright red.

My father noticed Nate, too. He leaned in toward me with a smile and whispered.

"My dear, I meant your *dog*."

* * *

Thank you!

Thank you for reading *Drop Dead Bread!*
If you enjoyed this book, please consider leaving a review or
rating on Amazon, Goodreads or the book review site of
your choice.

Look for Book 2 in this series:
Bread to Rights
and Book 3
Trouble You Don't Knead

Also by Victoria Kazarian

Bread to Rights - Laughing Loaf Bakery Mystery #2

Trouble You Don't Knead - Laughing Loaf Bakery Mystery #3

Traditional mystery

(Detectives Jimmy Ruiz and Dani Grasso):

Swift Horses Racing – Silicon Valley Murder Book 1

Across the Red Sky – Silicon Valley Murder Book 2

A Tree of Poison – Silicon Valley Murder Book 3

About Victoria Kazarian

Victoria Kazarian lives and writes in San Jose, California. After working for years as a Silicon Valley marketing professional, she taught high school English and actually owned a bread bakery of her own called The Laughing Loaf. When she's not writing, she enjoys baking artisan breads and forcing her children and dog to go on road trips to the Pacific Northwest.

See what she's up to at victoriakazarian.com

You can contact Victoria—or perhaps leave a message for Gracie Markley herself—at TheLaughingLoaf@gmail.com

Acknowledgments

Thank you to my copy editor and idea person, Honest Magpie, aka Armen Kazarian, for their hard work on this book and their honest critiques. And for bringing such an adorable chihuahua-basenji mix into our lives.

Thank you to the beta readers who made this book so much better: Chris Anderson, Rosanna Griffin and Debbie Cunningham.

To the phenomenal organization Sisters in Crime—SinC National, the Guppies group and the NorCal and Coastal Cruisers chapters—thank you. I would not be published if it weren't for you all.

Thank you to my husband, Pete, for your encouragement and for putting up with years of bread baking despite your gluten intolerance.

And to my dad Stan Vierk for being my biggest encourager to write and publish. He read my books on his Kindle not just once but multiple times—to make sure he remembered "who did it." He passed away at the age of eighty-eight while I was writing this book.

The Laughing Loaf Bakery Recipes

Morning Cinnamon Rolls

Total time from start to baked rolls: 3 hours
Makes a 9" x 12" pan of cinnamon rolls. Cut recipe in half to make less, with an 8" x 8" or 9" cake pan.

Ingredients

4-5 cups of all-purpose flour

2 tablespoons active dry yeast

2 cups warm water

2 tablespoons and 2/3 cup of brown sugar

2 teaspoons sea salt

¼ cup canola or safflower oil

¼ cup caramel ice cream topping

1. Mix the following things in a medium mixing bowl, then let sit for five minutes till mixture gets bubbly:

2 tablespoons active dry yeast

2 cups warm water

2 tablespoons brown sugar

2. Then add the above mixture and the following items to a large mixing bowl or stand mixer:

2 teaspoons sea salt

1/4 cup oil

4-1/4 cups flour

3. If you're mixing in a stand mixer, attach your dough hook and mix on low for about 5-6 minutes. The dough should start to gather around the hook. If it doesn't, add a bit more flour, a tablespoon at a time.

If you're kneading it by hand, mix the ingredients till well blended, then sprinkle flour on a flat, clean surface, dump the dough down on it and start kneading. Push the heels of your hands down into it and push forward, then flop the dough over on itself and do it again repeatedly, for about ten minutes. Knead the dough until it's almost firm (but not stiff) and is smooth and silky. If the dough spreads out too flat and limp, add a bit more flour (a tablespoon at a time).

4. **First Rise:** Now put the dough in a greased container and set it in a warm (not hot) place for an hour. Watch the time closely, so the dough doesn't overproof, which will make it flatten during baking. At the end of the hour, the dough should be doubled in size. Punch it down.

5. Grease a 9 x 12 pan (or cake pan if you've halved the recipe).

6. **The Filling:** In a saucepan, melt 1 stick of butter or margarine (1/2 cup). Add to it 1-1/2 tablespoons of cinna-

mon, 2/3 cup of brown sugar, and ¼ cup caramel ice cream topping.

Roll out the risen dough into big rectangle(s) about 1/4 inch thick. Spread the filling mixture on top of the rectangle. Cut each rectangle into long 1" wide strips and roll them up (not too tightly) and arrange them, spirals up, in the baking pan. The rolls will expand, so try to allow a half an inch or so between them.

7. **Second Rise:** Let the pan of rolled dough rise for 30 minutes. Meanwhile, preheat the oven to 350 degrees.

8. **The Bake:** Place the rolls on a rack in the *middle* of the oven, not too close to the top or bottom, for even baking. Bake for about 20 minutes, until the rolls are golden brown on top. It will be torture, but resist eating them until they've cooled for 15 minutes!

The Laughing Loaf Bakery Recipes

Gracie's Basic Scones

Time from start to baked, glazed scones: 40 minutes
Makes 8 scones

Ingredients
1-1/2 cups all-purpose flour
1/4 cup granulated sugar
1/2 teaspoon fine sea salt
1-½ teaspoons baking powder
½ teaspoon baking soda
3/4 stick (6 tablespoons) very cold butter, cut into cubes
1/2 cup buttermilk
2 large eggs, room temperature
1-1/2 teaspoons vanilla extract

Preheat oven to 400°F. Line a baking sheet with parchment paper.

1. In a large bowl, stir together thoroughly the dry ingredients: flour, sugar, salt, baking powder and baking soda.

2. Cut the butter into small cubes. Then mix it into the

dry mixture with a pastry cutter or (or bottom of a whisk) until the dough is roughly the texture of peas. Do no not touch the butter or dough with your warm hands. Keeping the butter cold will create nice layers in the scones.

3. In a separate large mixing bowl, mix together wet ingredients: buttermilk, one of the eggs, and vanilla extract. Make a well in the dry ingredients and dump in the wet ingredients; mix until just combined. **Do not** overmix, even if it looks shaggy and uneven.

Here's how to "laminate" your dough, to create layers for a light, flaky scone. Don't be intimidated; it's not that hard:

4. Dump the shaggy dough out onto your floured cutting board/work area. Avoid touching it excessively, you DO NOT want to melt the butter.

5. Shape dough into a square. Fold the square in half. Use a rolling pin to roll it out till it's a square again, about ½" thick. Turn it 90 degrees and fold it over, then roll it out again. Repeat this turning and rolling process once more until you end up with the ½" thick square. Nudge the corners with the rolling pin until it's a rough round.

6. Using a sharp knife, cut the round into 8 triangular wedges.

7. Beat the other egg and brush it lightly over the top of each scone. Place the cut wedges onto a baking sheet. Bake for 12 minutes or until lightly browned.

To glaze your baked scones, mix 1 cup of powdered sugar with 2-1/2 tablespoons of milk and 1 teaspoon of vanilla (or 1 teaspoon grated lemon zest), till smooth. Brush on the scones while they're still warm.

At The Laughing Loaf, Gracie freezes the cut, unbaked scones so she can pull them out and bake them when she needs them. Cover the scones tightly with cling/stretch wrap on a baking sheet. The frozen scones will keep nicely in the freezer for a month. They'll require a couple more minutes of baking when frozen.

***

Are you in a book club?

Are you in a book club?
Interested in reading any of The Laughing Loaf Bakery
Mysteries? I'd love to appear at your book club virtually - or
in person, if you're in the San Francisco Bay Area.
Contact me at thelaughingloaf@gmail.com